JOSEPH DARLING   er,
England. He was no   h
Prize for Short Fictic   ie
Manchester Review of Doors since 2016.

The Girl Beneath the Ice is his first published novel. Find
him on Twitter at @Joe_Darlo.

THE GIRL
BENEATH
THE ICE

JOSEPH DARLINGTON

Northodox Press Ltd
Maiden Greve, Malton,
North Yorkshire, YO17 7BE

This edition 2021

1

First published in Great Britain
by Northodox Press Ltd 2021

ISBN: 978-1-8383430-9-5

This book is set in Sabon LT Std

For Kinga - with love and squalor.

Cast of Characters

William Farringdon – patriarch of the Farringdons. A retired businessman who came the country for peace and quiet, hoping it would cure his wife's alcoholism.

Lucas "Luke" Farringdon – son of William and boyfriend of Tasha. A popular boy at school, sporty and confident. Hopelessly in love with Tasha.

Tasha Bancroft – a popular girl at school, albeit with a cruel streak. Her mother ran away when she was a baby. The girl beneath the ice.

Mrs Bancroft – the headteacher of the local comprehensive and grandmother of Tasha. A disciplinarian and cynic still heartbroken by her daughter running away.

Inspector Dafydd Todor – a hapless inspector, recently promoted as a way to banish him to Avon Murray. Terminally unlucky and suffering with imposter syndrome.

Todd Morrow – the local forester and a recluse. Haunted by something that happened to him in the city a few years earlier, shunning society and living deep in the woods. He is the prime suspect in Tasha's murder.

Frigite "Frigg" McBride – schoolmates with Luke and Tasha, and often a victim of the latter's bullying. She practices black magic and recently placed a curse on Tasha.

Chapter One

William Farringdon

The snow stopped falling. It had been coming down for almost three weeks. Sometimes it fell like a heavy rain, pelting the too-white surface of the Earth. Sometimes it drifted down in peaceful clusters. Both were insidious. The snow fell, and it kept falling, until the people of Avon Murray began to wonder if it would ever stop.

The thin white blanket had been pleasant at first. It was January, and the mild Christmas just gone had made many oldies nostalgic for the deep snows of the past. On that first frosty morning the slopes of Baybold's Park were jammed with sledges, parents in parkers sipped from hot chocolates, and cheeks glowed as red as the hearths.

On the second day, the snow grew heavier. The children stayed inside. Concerns were raised over the gritters, and Snake Pass was said to have become impassable.

From the third day onwards, official advice warned everyone to stay indoors. Icy winds had been reported only four valleys over, powerful enough to blow the elderly off their feet. Icicles grew on eyelashes. Those who could stocked up and the supermarkets soon emptied.

By the end of that first week, Avon Murray was frozen solid. No-one left their homes and even if they had done, there was nowhere to go to. The town was miles from anywhere with the bridges to the surrounding villages iced over.

The Farringdon family were the same as any other in Avon Murray when it came to the ice. Their big house on the hill was no warmer than the cottages below. Their high standing did nothing to keep them dry, nor did their unassuming wealth keep hunger from creeping in.

William Farringdon, the family patriarch, began each morning by building a fire in the living room, the kitchen, and in his wife's bedroom. He would eat breakfast with his son, Lucas, while staring out of the frosted windows at the ever-falling snow. A tin of dogmeat would serve for Scout's breakfast and then, for a few quiet hours, he might sit and read, hoping the next time he looked outside that the day might have cleared, the sun returned, and the thaw finally begun.

Which explained why he was out that day, despite all the weather warnings. William had been waiting with his nose pushed against the glass for the snows to subside. Just for a second, he pleaded. Just long enough for a turn around the garden.

And so, when the snow stopped falling, William pulled on his wellies. Warnings be damned, he was going for a walk.

'Come on Scout!' he whistled, feeling the springer spaniel push past his legs. She bounded out into the cold.

He zipped up his jacket, catching on his moustache, and screwed on his flatcap. The freezing wind wouldn't stop him. Scout leaped through the snow drifts, thrashing wildly like a hooked marlin. Her tongue lolled happily.

'Dad,' Lucas called from an upstairs window. 'What are you doing outside? Are you okay?'

'Just taking a turn, son.'

William waved his umbrella in salutation.

'Shouldn't be too long. The snow's stopped.'

Lucas peered at the still-grey skies, searching for a few lone flakes, anything foretelling of danger. As he saw his father wading through into the drifts, heading to the garden gate, Lucas called out again.

'Where are you going?'

William paused. He hadn't yet considered where.

'I suppose I'll take the riverside route,' he called. 'Follow the Highwood Basin down to the Millpond, then up to the town. See how things stand. It's not too difficult a walk.'

'Okay,' Lucas sounded nervous. 'Well take care.'

'Will do. And keep quiet while I'm gone, Lucas. Your mother's not well.'

'Yes dad.'

And with that William walked out past his creaking cast-iron gate, onto the bridleway, and away across the wooded hillside in the direction of town.

Living outside of Avon Murray had its benefits. The small-town chatter-tired William tremendously. It was the one thing which made him long for the city again. That and the bank holiday backpackers.

He was a man easily frustrated, and had to remind himself

at times that, despite moving out to the   countryside for peace and quiet, the countryside was under no obligation to provide it to him.

In summer, Avon Murray could be as busy as Piccadilly Gardens on a Saturday.

Yet, for all its peace, the Farringdon's house, perched high in the steep valley, nestled in woods, had an oppressiveness of its own to contend with.

'Come on, Scout. Come on!' William called.

They had turned off the road where the path was indistinguishable now, sunk in snow.

They waded into a meadow.

Scout was leaping and turning in the air again, wearing herself out after long days without exercise. William brought her in close to him, aware that there could be danger beneath the snow. Dead animals, perhaps. Poisonous plants. Rough ground.

'You stick by me, Scout,' he patted his leg. 'You stay close, girl. I need you here, by me.'

Scout, tongue waggling, breath heavy, obeyed.

'It's good to be out, eh girl? We've been cooped up too long. We've missed the air.'

As they walked, one trotting now at the heel of the other, the clouds even seemed to part and the sun, unseen for three weeks, threatened to once again show its face.

William was by no means a sun seeker. In fact, by constitution he was a lover of cold and rugged climates. The family's holidays, when they had taken holidays, had been to places like Norway, Iceland, the Alps, and

Russia. No, he was no stranger to snow and ice. Even now he found the icy wind which chapped his cheeks invigorating. No, it was being trapped inside which was the problem.

The summer just passed, his daughter, Jo, had left for university. They had not heard from her since and William knew why. It was Helen, his wife and Jo's mother. In recent years her drinking had driven her almost to the point of being bedridden. She slept through the morning, then took her wine, then gin. She'd withdrawn entirely to the confines of her bedroom.

Somehow, the less they saw of Helen, the more of a presence she had in the house.

The Farringdons were always quiet, not wanting to wake her, never knowing when she was asleep. At dinner, William would set a place just in case she came down. She never did.

The last time she came down was after four months locked in her bedroom. They had not set a place for her. As she fumbled her way into the kitchen and stood, shaking, leaning over the three seated figures who trembled in turn, watching her with open mouths, she looked to where her place had once been set and saw nothing. Then she broke down crying.

'You have no place for me!' William remembered her screaming. 'You all want me dead!'

Since then he'd always set the table, just in case. Although, since then, she'd never come down to dinner again. Jo, always sensitive, always hyperaware of undertones, would spend her dinners in silence, staring at the empty place. William wanted to chide her for it but couldn't find the words. Instead he just sighed and made small talk with Lucas.

William knew that when Jo went to uni she wouldn't be back. Not for a long while at least.

'Come on, Scoutie! Here we are.'

William opened the gate to the Roundy-Hill, as the family called it. It was a round lump sticking out from the steep field. Perhaps an old Viking burial mound? Lucas had laughed at that. He played there with his friends, raiding imaginary villages and racing down to the river with homemade longboats.

They had all played up there back in the past; William, Jo and baby Lucas, all sledding down the Roundy-Hill. In the snow it looked rounder than ever.

'Remember Scout, eh?'

William pointed up the slope

'You were just a little puppy. You were good at sledding though. Put you on the front of Jo's sled, we did. Remember?'

He ruffled Scout's head with his hand. Warm wet snow was melting in her fur. 'I don't suppose you'd be so good at sledding now, Scout. And I don't suppose I'd be much good either. We'll leave that to the young ones, eh?'

Scout looked up the Roundy-Hill, her eyes darting. Perhaps she remembered, William thought. Perhaps.

He didn't know where it had all gone wrong with Helen.

He felt he ought to accept some of the blame onto himself,

but then what that responsibility was had never been defined. Instead he felt only an abstract and generalised guilt. If he could find some reason to be guilty, he thought, then at least that would alleviate the burden from Jo and Lucas, and perhaps even Helen herself. If he could take it all on his shoulders somehow, then he would.

At times this was all he wanted. Not to end her drinking, or have things back as they once were, but only to have it made clear to all of them that it was his fault. That *he* was to blame, and he alone. But William didn't know how. One dream seemed as unreachable as the other.

When he thought back to their good times they were always mired in some kind of sorrow. Everything was always a travesty. Every good and happy moment a prelude to heartbreak.

A memory had come back to William as he gazed out into the snow, of a winter over a decade ago, when Helen had drank too much on Christmas as she always had.

There had been a fight on Christmas evening. William had slept on the sofa. Helen in the spare room that would, in time, become her bedroom. Neither slept in their bed. The next day, they awoken around eleven in the morning and, each filled with the same remorse and longing, they worked their way to that big bed of theirs and fell asleep there together. They slept right through to the evening.

That evening they came downstairs and sat together in front of the television. William opened another bottle of wine and they drank, a blanket wrapped around them, watching old movies and picking at leftovers.

As he thought about it now his heart filled up. He remembered it as one of their most wonderful times together. He thought of it when he couldn't bear her anymore.

He thought of it to get him through, to have something that may, perhaps one day, happen again. But no matter how he tried to forget, he couldn't. Because, as they lay together there, happy in their way, drinking and watching movies, they had left the young Jo and Lucas at their grandma's house.

They had dropped them off Christmas morning, promising to return in an hour. When they finally came back it was the day after Boxing Day.

They never called. Never explained. How could they?

And so, every good memory William had was somehow lined with guilt. He understood why Jo had left, and why she never called. Lucas was harder to understand. Popular at school. A good sportsman. His girlfriend even a bit of a looker.

'Come on, girl. Up over there!'

They had reached the boundary where the fields gave way to the woods. Scout leapt over the stile and William followed. She liked this bit of the walk and would normally need calling back, running as she did among the trees, furrowing every mound with her nose, looking for things to chew and chase. The woods were empty now. Black wood and whiteness against a grey sky.

William let her snuffle and walked on down the muddy path to the river, lost in his own thoughts.

'Lucas is an odd one,' he said out loud.

He spoke partly to himself, partly to Scout, and what remained into the empty air.

'All the rest of us out here are muddled up with grief and guilt. We're all tied in knots. Lucas, our boy Lucas, he seems to cut right through it all. He skims right over the top. There's nothing troubling the boy, I swear it! In the middle of all of this… emotional wreckage, he just carries on…'

Scout ran up now, a branch carried in her too-small mouth. 'Lucas is doing better than all of us, eh Scoutie?' William sniffed.

He prised the branch from her mouth and snapped it in half, dropping half and raising half to throw. Scout barked, giddy.

William, aware that the river was coming up ahead, aimed the branch up the hill and flung with all his might. It flew out over the bushes and into the trees beyond. Scout dived after it as he wiped his hands on his trousers.

'Perhaps its good genes,' he laughed, grimly.

William was only too aware of his ancestral endowment. Genes sat on Farringdon men like destiny. His father, for all his faults, was a bright and charming man. His mother had been an alcoholic. It was the same with his grandparents, and now him.

Lucas, as young and fancy-free as he appeared to be, was nevertheless stricken by love. William knew the sight of it. Not the joy and excitement he'd seen on other loved-up faces, but the family look of barely contained panic. A look busy with wandering thoughts.

Desperation. He was falling for young, what's her name?

The wet dog bounded back with the branch.

Ah, that was it, Tasha. Young Tasha Barcroft.

He lifted the branch again and launched it, this time towards a clearing. The valley was narrowing further and further, and the river visible now, snaking down the frozen valley floor. A light dust of snow lay on its surface like icing sugar on a Victoria sponge.

She seemed a nice girl, that Tasha, if a bit strong-headed. If she could put it to good use she would certainly get on in life.

William watched Scout disappear into the bushes again. He knew, of course, of Tasha's ill providence. Her mother was a tear away. She'd gotten pregnant at fifteen and abandoned Tasha to go party in the city. Tasha had been raised by her grandmother, Mrs Barcroft. He didn't know her first name.

Mrs Barcroft was the head of the local secondary school. She was Lucas' current headteacher, and Tasha's too for that matter. By Lucas' account she was something of an old battleaxe. But perhaps she feared genetic destiny, too.

'If the world is already written,' William rubbed at the ice beading on his moustache. 'In God's great book up above, then the genes that bring those two together will make of them what it's made of us. But then, one can't live if one only sees what's written. One must have faith. One must have hope, eh Scoutie?'

Scout wandered up to William. She dropped her branch before reaching him. It was her subtle way of showing she'd had enough of the fetching game.

William walked on. The gnawed branch sat there in the mud. The saliva on it was cooling, and would soon be ice.

Scout stuck close to William's heel as they reached the steepest and most narrow part of the valley. Here, a committed walker could ascend, but a descent without ropes would be impossible. Trees clung to the narrow channels between rocks, warped and twisted by the wind.

The path moved in and out in serpentine motions beside the riverbank.

Sometimes William could see right out over it. It was clear and somewhere, right down at the bottom, a few resilient weeds rippled in the water. The river was still moving then, deep beneath the ice. Although even down there it was slushy; only a degree or two above zero.

As the path twisted away from the river again, William called to Scout.

'No swimming today, eh girl?'

In the summer this was her favourite part of the walk.

'You're a merdog in summer, aren't you? Well if you went in now, my lovely, we'd never get you out again.'

Scout wagged her tail, happy to be talked to, sniffing at the air as she went. Her eyes peered around, searching for signs of life, anything other than the monochrome winter.

Then, without warning, Scout stopped.

William raised an eyebrow and stopped too, not recognising this behaviour, unprecedented in the twelve years he'd had her.

'Is everything alright, Scout?'

Scout's eyes darted, forward and back along the riverbank, nostrils flaring as she sniffed the cold air. Slowly, with William in pursuit, she edged forward, nose to the ground.

They crossed over a patch of dead brambles and then climbed the rocky outcrop which overlooked a pool.

Scout, looking out, sniffed a few more times. Confirming the scent, she barked.

'What is it, girl?'

Her barks echoed, clear and percussive through the frozen silence. They weren't yelps of panic or excitement. Not even of warning. She was drawing his attention. Perhaps drawing attention in general; to something she sensed out there.

He lifted his hand over his eyes and peered.

'It's no good, girl.'

He looked down as she barked.

'I don't know what you're getting at. I can't see anything.'

The barking continued.

William decided that he needed a better view. He made for the bridge.

The footbridge was stone, held together only by moss and time. It was the sort of bridge that weather and walking boots should, by rights, have worn away to nothing but, perhaps bound by the glue of tradition, it still stood as firm, if not firmer, than when it was first erected.

William strode out on to it and looked down.

He saw what Scout had been barking about.

'Oh my God,' William gasped, his breath catching in his throat.

It was a girl frozen beneath the ice.

She seemed untouched, undamaged, unhurt even. Her long red-blonde hair splayed out from her head, as if caught in a breeze. Her eyes open, lips ever so slightly parted, and trapped in a state of constant amazement. Her skin was pale white with touches of red as it had been before she was frozen.

The ice was unnaturally clear. Perfect, like a window that she might open and step out of at any moment.

As if she might step out of the ice and laugh, revealing it all to be a joke.

And it wasn't just any girl. A girl who had been in their house dozens and dozens of times. His son's girlfriend. Granddaughter of Mrs Barcroft. Tasha Barcroft.

Tasha, who he was still unsure of. Tasha, who his son loved. Frozen beneath the ice.

William looked down at her, as did Scout. The dog barked, but William remained silent, not knowing what to do.

Chapter Two

William Farringdon

'Quiet, girl! Quiet!' William patted Scout's back. 'I know. I know.'

They stared down at the girl beneath the ice.

As she hung there, locked in glass, they stifled an urge to jump in and rescue her. She seemed so close, only four feet below them, and she looked so alive.

William gathered himself. Now the first moments of shock had passed he found his eyes desperately searching for ways into the pool. The entire river was frozen. From what he had seen the ice was thick. The only glacial movement was right down at the bottom.

It was likely that the ice that held Tasha Barcroft was solid from surface to riverbed.

Perhaps he could walk out over the ice? Perhaps it would hold him? But then, do what? Once he was there we could hardly lift her out himself.

But she looked so alive. He refused to think of her as a dead body. He could only think of her as a girl in need of rescue. Scout whimpered.

As he looked down from the stone bridge and felt, with

a terrible shudder, the tell-tale tingle of snowflakes landing on his skin. He looked up and, sure enough, falling down between the black and lifeless trees came little gusts of snow.

In his haste to get out of the house he'd not checked the weather. All that had come from the radio for the past two and a half weeks were emergency warnings telling him not to leave the house. He'd left too soon.

He'd learned enough these past few days to know how quick a little powder turned to freezing winds and sleet.

'Troublesome stuff, Scout.'

William scanned the skies above before gazing back down at Tasha.

'We're in trouble, no doubt. All of us perhaps. What to do, what to do...'

He patted his coat and felt for any square-shaped bumps. Finding one, he pulled off a glove and, with pink fingers, unzipped his pocket and removed his phone.

'Thank God I'd brought it, eh?' he chuckled, an edge of hysteria creeping into his voice.

Waiting only to gather his breath, William dialled in the emergency number and held the phone to his ear.

He waited. Nothing at first. Then, inevitably, exactly as he'd predicted, he heard three pips: bip-bip-bip...

He looked down at the phone and saw the call had been disconnected. William was used to having no signal out here in Avon Murray, but it was rare that emergency calls didn't connect.

The emergency numbers were supposed to be on an alternative network. They were supposed to reach into every nook and cranny, covering the whole country. But no system was perfect. Down here in the depths of the river valley even the emergency numbers could find nothing to hold on to. The valley was locked up, even the air, in ice and obscurity.

'Right, girl,' William stirred himself. 'This is more than we can handle. We need to call in reinforcements. It looks like we'll have to carry on up this path. We should get out from under these trees. Ideally, right out of the valley. The signal should come back then. Are you ready, girl? Come on!'

William patted his thigh as he turned and strode. The path twisted up around the trees, disappearing and reappearing before finally showing a way out of the valley. The pair moved at a trot.

Then, up ahead, they saw movement. William's eyes darted through the trees, seeing only black and white dashes. Scout, running slightly ahead, began to bark.

William started running. He'd not run in years. His body rebelled. But Scout was barking and his adrenaline was up.

Somewhere out there, he was sure, was the killer. He didn't know why he thought this, nor why he thought it with such certainty, but in his guts, he knew. He ran, shoulders and legs aching, heart pounding in his chest. He ran.

The black trees swung by. The figure, whoever they were, had strafed sideways off the path ahead of them. Scout barked and William saw a bramble patch swaying with the murderer's retreat.

'Hey!' he shouted, hearing his own breathlessness wrasping in his throat. 'Come back! Stop! Murderer! Murderer!'

He reached the bend where the figure had darted away.

His blood rising behind his eyes, William had to stop. If he kept going it would be his end. His old heart wasn't what it once was. But there, as he stood coughing and heaving in air, William saw him.

The figure had stopped, a dark green raincoat wrapping his form, gripping an ankle as if it were twisted. Perhaps he'd caught it on the undergrowth, William thought. Or perhaps it bore the marks of a struggle, the marks of murder.

'Murderer!' he called again. Scout barked.

The figure turned and William saw his face. No mystery this, he would recognise the man anywhere. Todd Morrow.

'I see you Todd Morrow!' he cried out, raising a finger in accusation. 'I've seen you!'

The heavily bearded Morrow looked like a fox scenting hounds, terror was visible in his wide eyes, even through the twisted foliage. Hunted eyes. Guilty eyes.

'You can run,' William called. 'But I've seen you. You'll hang for this Todd Morrow! You should hope the police find you before we do.'

The green-hooded figure crumpled up, as if William's words were a bullet punching his belly. Then, just as quickly as he'd come, he was gone.

William shook his head on the verge of tears.

He would like to think it was the pain, seeping up his legs and into his chest. Pain from exercise long neglected. He would like too, to think that the tears were for Tasha Barcroft, the poor frozen girl, and the horrible fate that had befallen her.

But, as he looked down at the lolling tongue of Scout,

and at his own hastily-tied walking boots, he knew that some of his tears were for himself. He cried for his own poor family, to be caught up in all this. And he cried for the ugliness of murder, and for the end of the quiet that had held him so long, frozen in his unhappiness, things never getting better, but never worse either.

'Come on, boy!' He whispered eventually to Scout. 'Let's get out of this godforsaken valley. I need signal. I need a strong drink.'

They turned and made their way up the steep and snaking path.

William was limping now. Scout stuck close by him, eyes peering keenly through the brush and black branches, seeking out the dangers that threatened her master.

Under his breath, William cursed Todd Morrow.

He knew Morrow the way that all respectable people in Avon Murray knew him; as the town hermit. Once a teenage heartthrob, he fell into drugs and music, leaving for a short time to go to the city only to return, smaller, chastened, and unwilling to speak about his experiences there. It was widely accepted that something terrible had happened. Perhaps Morrow himself had done something unforgivable?

Either way, he had been snubbed by the town. The only work he could get was with the Forestry Commission, in woodlands maintenance as Avon Murray's resident forester. The position suited his newfound fear of human contact, and within weeks he was living as a hermit in the woods. He grew a long beard and emerged only once a week for supplies. He spoke to no one, and left as silently as he came.

Parents told their children to stay away from him. Teenagers told scary stories and dared each other to approach his shack at night. It was widely assumed that he was insane.

'We should have known,' William shook his head, speaking not to Scout now but to himself. 'To let a wild man, live among us… to have harboured a deranged lunatic within our midst…'

In the city, William knew, such men as Morrow were locked away before they even had a chance to hurt others. Out there they let them run free. Things were looser there. It was one of the things he liked about the place. But now they were paying for it. They were all guilty for this, he told himself. Not just that monster in green.

The snow fell thicker now and in the dark recesses of William's mind he saw an image of Morrow tangled up in thorns and frozen stiff. Perhaps, he reflected with a shudder, nature would take care of her own?

White clumps were falling by the time they reached the gate. Scout hopped the fence and William whistled to her, drawing her back from the ice-washed road.

No-one would be driving in this weather. No-one would even be outside, other than him. But still he must exhibit a respect for the road. It was a laxness around rules that had led to this after all, he thought.

In an alley between two bungalows, William Farringdon finally found signal. Clutching his wet dog close to his leg, he rang the emergency number and laughed as he heard a voice.

Chapter Three

Inspector Todor

Inspector Dafydd Todor sipped tentatively from his coffee cup.

He was sat in the back of a patrol car, too aware that driving in Avon Murray could mean cobbles at any time. He took small, rapid sips, staring out of the window at the redbrick terraces and ivy-clad cottages rushing by.

'Now what I don't understand is what *he* was doing out there,' said a police officer in the front seat. 'The town's supposed to be on lockdown, isn't it?'

'No respect,' the driver muttered under his breath.

He, like Inspector Todor, was a recent transfer to the department. He took Avon Murray's casual approach to the law as a personal affront.

'I mean,' the other officer continued. 'There shouldn't have been anyone out of their homes at all, and here we have at least *three* people all caught up in a murder? It doesn't make sense. All very suspicious, if you ask me.'

Inspector Todor could hear by the officer's tone that he was looking for confirmation. Sighing, he took a sip and turned to the officer in front.

'It makes perfect sense, Berkeley,' he swallowed. 'When better to commit murder than when you can guarantee everyone's locked up indoors?'

He placed his hand over the top of his cup. As they hit cobbles, he felt the hot liquid on his downturned palm.

'And what's this about *at least three*?'

'Well,' Berkeley shrugged and counted on his fingers: 'Farringdon's one. Morrow's two. And the girl makes three.'

'I see.'

Todor went back to staring out of the window.

'Just for the record, Berkeley, when we're listing people "involved" in a murder, we don't tend to include the victim.'

The car swung left at a roundabout. Inspector Todor tried to hold the case in his mind, but found the details slipping away. Like everyone else, the long freeze had kept him indoors, away from action, locked in a state of semi-hibernation. He found himself dreaming instead of the small towns of his youth; Porth and Llwyncelyn, half an hour North of Cardiff.

He thought of the six-foot drifts back in '77. They were like sheer cliffs of powder to the five-year-old Dafydd. He remembered the trucks still chugging away through the falling snow. Constant strikes, three-day weeks, and still everything ticked on. He wondered if they were all getting soft, or was it really worse now?

Todor felt like a man out of his time. He'd ended up in Avon Murray through a series of face-saving compromises, all designed to restore some kind of dignity to a man who everyone recognised as broken.

He'd spent his whole life in Glamorgan, policing. He had a wife and kids. Had, in the past tense. As he watched the rest get promoted over him, disappear to big cities and glamorous assignments, Todor kept on walking the beat, every year getting older, less secure, and less capable of chasing down a shoplifter or striding with confidence into a domestic.

He'd taken to drinking. His kids left home. His wife left him. Then, when he was heard at the Christmas party making a particularly bitter and off-colour joke, it was decided that the respect due to the man's loyalty no longer outweighed his threat as a potential liability.

The higher ups decided to do something, and so they promoted him.

Dafydd Todor was finally made an Inspector, at the age of forty-six, on the premise that he would move far away from Wales and, ideally, never return.

He couldn't be sure whether the other police of Avon Murray knew about his past. They acted as if they didn't, as if he were a legitimate inspector. He liked it that way. It had helped him to sober up, and to regain some self-respect. But still the threat of his past sat in his belly

It was a heavy burden of guilt, and so he was keen to do things purely by the book. No risks. He couldn't take chances.

He was sure that one day his past would catch up to him. Eventually it caught up with everyone, he knew.

The car pulled to a halt beside the ginnel, skidding a few inches along the ice before stopping. The snow fell in clumps now, fist-thick and drifting, slow and inevitable. The ginnel led behind the row of bungalows to the steep river valley beyond.

'Alright.'

Inspector Todor swallowed the last of his coffee, leaving the empty cup jammed in the car door. The officers stepped out, shielding their faces from the wind. The town was under weather warning for good reason.

As they stepped into the ginnel, Todor spotted the active duty sergeant at the other end. She was talking with the flustered figure of William Farringdon.

'Inspector Todor, this is William Farringdon, he called in the-'

'I know who he is, sergeant,' Todor nodded. 'Mr Farringdon is a respected member of the community. Are you okay, sir? Do you feel quite well?'

'Quite well,' William nodded.

The black and white springer spaniel sat at his feet and whimpered. She was shivering.

'That's a lovely dog you have there, sir,' Todor smiled. 'I have one of my own; a Dalmatian-cross, name of Willie. What's this one called?'

William looked down at the dog, his chapped fingers rustling in her wet fur.

'She's called Scout. After Kinder, you know.'

'Ah, so you're a rambling man?' the Inspector nodded. 'I've taken a few turns up and down Kinder myself. I suppose that would explain what you were doing out in the middle of a snowstorm.'

'I just wanted some fresh air,' William sighed. A darkness

was gathering in his eyes. They no longer focused on the objects around him. He was becoming maudlin, Todor knew, just as all witnesses did once the initial shock had passed and the weight of their encounter began to impress itself upon their understanding.

'Well how's about we get you warmed up and dry?'

The Inspector gestured to the officer beside them.

'I'll walk you to the car. You two,' he called out to the other officers. 'You get down to the cordon by the river. See if you can't organise a party to go and bring in our boyo.'

'Yes, sir.'

Their heels clicked.

Perhaps in parody, Todor thought. His stomach twisted with guilt. He led William away by the arm.

'So just to clarify, sir; you were out walking your dog, getting some "*fresh air*" as you put it, when you came upon the body of a girl, one Tasha Barcroft, frozen in the river?'

William nodded. He walked with a stoop now, like an old man.

Only ten years older than himself if that, Todor thought.

'And upon seeing the body in the river you began to call for help?'

'No,' William shook his head. 'I wanted to call the police but there was no signal. I started walking up here and then-'

'-and then you saw a Mr Morrow escaping through the trees. Running with,' Todor flipped out his notebook and checked the details. 'A green raincoat on and a wild look in his eyes.'

William nodded.

'That is correct. Exactly as you say.'

'Any reason you didn't shout for help then, sir?' the Inspector asked.

'No,' William shook his head.

Then, pausing, he raised his eyes to the heavy clouds and knitted his eyebrows.

'Or perhaps I did? I *was* shouting I think. I can't remember *what* I was shouting. It happened so fast.'

The Inspector fixed William with a quizzical look. He noticed the gentleman couldn't meet his eye.

He patted him on the back; 'Well, that should be enough for now, sir. We've enough to go on there. Why don't you get into the patrol car and our officer here will take you back to the station? We'll get you both warm and dry; you and Scout here.'

'Thank you.'

William smiled joylessly before ducking his head into the car. He took a seat in the back, as if he were a criminal. Todor thought of noting this down, this unconscious sign of guilt, before realising that he too had chosen that seat for the ride down.

We are all criminals here, perhaps, he thought to himself.

As he walked back down the ginnel, he flipped through his notebook. He was already sketching out background details connecting the victim with suspects. Todd Morrow was indeed a wild man, living on the outer bounds of society. He would know these woods as any normal man would know their own home. Yet, in terms of connections, William Farringdon did seem well placed.

Inspector Todor looked at his notes. Arrows from one name to another, a whole quiver of them. Tasha Barcroft linked to Mrs Barcroft, the headteacher of William Farringdon's son's school. There was also a link, albeit a more tentative one, between Tasha and the son himself.

That Farringdon was the one to find the body was, he thought, a huge coincidence. But then was it? In small towns everybody's connected, and coincidences, no matter how large, are not always meaningful.

The only one *not* connected was Todd Morrow. And he had the boyos out after him already. Todor had seen enough murder to know that usually the most obvious killer was the right one.

Once they had Todd Morrow in custody he'd be better placed to read his character. Ultimately it would come down to that. Well, until they could gather forensics anyway.

As the Inspector paced down the curving path towards the river he could sense the stillness in the air. The valley was silent. Other than the crunching of his boots on snow there wasn't a voice nor a scuffle of movement in the whole deep dip.

At one end he could see the yellow jackets of his officers, fanning out and moving through the valley, searching for their man. At the other he saw a clearing where a glistening wall of white fell heavy on the ground. Below were more yellow jackets, the frozen river pool and the stone bridge arching over it.

'The bridge is too fragile for a crane?' He shouted to the officers as he bounded down the path.

'Yes, sir,' one nodded. 'Even if we could get the machinery down the slope, there's nowhere here stable enough to hold it.'

Todor stepped onto the bridge himself. It was indeed old. His boots slipped a little on the moss. Its walls were low, suggesting that a loss of balance would not easily be stabilised. A dangerous bridge, then.

'Keep your men off the bridge,' he said.

The officer nodded enthusiastically. Todor's eyes narrowed, unsure if she was mocking him.

He looked down on the body. He sniffed.

He wasn't normally one for appraising the dead; he would check what he needed to and then get away as soon as possible. The dead haunted his dreams sometimes. It was part of the job.

But there, looking down at the girl beneath the ice, his lifelong feelings about the dead were suddenly different. He felt light. Peaceful almost.

The girl had a look of such beatific calm it was as if she weren't dead at all. Or perhaps death didn't matter to her? She was fine with passing. At total peace with moving on. She looked out at Todor with lazily-lidded eyes and he felt the power of death. Death, the great forgiver. One day he too would be at peace.

'She's unnerving isn't she, sir?' the officer on the riverbank said.

'Very,' Todor nodded. 'The sooner we get her out of

there the better.'

With difficulty, he dragged his eyes away from the body and inspected the ice around it. There was no loose snow on the surface, suggesting that the river had frozen solid from the ground up.

This meant two things, both of which ruled out rescue approaches. Firstly, it meant that the canopy above was thick enough to keep off every bit of snow from the past two weeks of storms. This ruled out helicopter access.

Secondly, it suggested that the water was frozen right to the bottom. The sub-zero temperatures probably continued deep into the river bed. This ruled out breaking up the ice and floating her over to the bank.

If the whole thing was frozen, top to bottom, she'd need digging out. This was careful work, and could take days. They had to do it properly, or risk damaging the body. It was that, or waiting until she thawed, or... well, nothing else really.

'Riley! Kivilahti!' Inspector Todor called out to the two police patrolling the scene. 'Are you up for trying something out for me?'

'Trying something out, sir?' Riley asked.

Kivilahti raised a quizzical eyebrow as Todor stepped off the bridge.

'You see, as far as I can fathom,' Todor gestured. 'This ice here is formed from the bottom up. That should make the whole river one solid block of ice. Following that reasoning, you two should be able to walk quite safely over to the spot where the girl is buried and tell me how much ice there is between her body and the surface.'

The police officers chewed their lips. Todor rubbed his hands together.

'Once we know that, we can get some special equipment ordered – picks and things, you know – and we'll have our lass out of here in no time.'

The two officers looked at each other.

'Alright sir, if you're sure.'

Todor nodded.

With that, the two officers lowered themselves down off the riverbank and on to the ice. They placed their first steps lightly, expecting any moment to hear a crack, but nothing came. Instead, the ice held firm.

Pleased with their first steps, the two walked out on the ice. They swung their arms a little to steady themselves, the ice was still very slippery after all, but after one step, then another, then another, their confidence grew. Riley turned back to Todor with a grin on his face. The Inspector gave him a thumbs-up in response.

They walked out, over the ice, moving slowly but determinedly toward their destination.

Then, suddenly, and without warning, they heard a bang.

It echoed through the black trees and was followed, almost immediately after, by a horrible whoosh.

The ice under both officer's feet gave way. It fell instantly, all in one rushing movement, plunging their lower halves into freezing water. The pain must have been like a thousand knives stabbing into their exposed flesh.

The officers screamed and panicked. They grabbed for

the ice behind them; the safe ice, from whence they came.

Todor, eyes wide with panic, watched the officers struggling. For a moment all he could feel was guilt. Then, snapping to attention, he dove out across the ice towards them.

He flattened himself out, spreading his body weight.

He was horribly aware that if the ice cracked beneath him, he wouldn't just lose his legs beneath it. He'd sink, head-first, under its iron-hard surface. A monstrous way to die. He reached out both his hands, desperate to reach the officers as they flailed and yelled.

'Help!' he cried out to the heavens. 'Officers down! Officers down!'

Finally, one of his hands reached one of theirs. He felt his other grasped, moments after. Heaving, heaving, he pulled them up on to the ice to safety.

Frostbite would be sinking in already. He needed to get them to a hospital as soon as possible. He grabbed for his walkie-talkie, calling for back up, calling for help, any at all.

He heard then that they'd caught Todd Morrow. He heard that Berkeley was on his way back to the crime scene and, no time to wait for an ambulance, that he'd drive them to A&E himself. But all he could think of was the ice. There was no way it could have given way. He was certain of its thickness, of its safety. Otherwise, how was the girl suspended there like that?

He thought of the girl's lazy eyes. Of her infinite calm.

You will be guilty, Dafydd Todor, she seemed to say. *Guilty until you are dead.*

Chapter Four

Mrs Barcroft

'Send him up.'

She replaced the receiver and straightened her cardigan. From her office window she looked out across bike sheds and playing fields, all covered with snow. Her office was situated at the top of the science block. It crouched there, overhanging, like an eyrie.

It took precisely six and a half minutes for a visitor to walk from the reception to her office. She used the time to straighten her things and ready herself.

She put on a presentable, yet stern and unflinching face. Slid the piles of unfinished work into a draw. Paperwork was always the bane of her job and yet, she insisted on it.

She hid the excess away, leaving only a reasonable pile. Enough to signify that she was busy.

There, on her desk, was a set of double portraits. To the left, her daughter, Jennifer, and to the right, her granddaughter, Tasha. How similar they looked, she thought. And yet neither with much of a likeness to herself.

The photo of her daughter was taken when she was fourteen years, showing a well-turned-out girl, with pigtails and a winning smile. She wore braces, just as Tasha had at that age.

Mrs Barcroft raised her hand to her lips and felt the dentures beneath. Perhaps if they'd had braces back in her youth…

She ran a finger down the faces. Tasha's photo was taken only a year ago. Fifteen going on sixteen with the same smile as her mother. A look, Mrs Barcroft thought grimly, of innocence about to be crushed.

Crushed? No. Perhaps *dispensed with* would have been better.

She worried about her granddaughter. Tasha had the same turbulent streak her mother had. The blood of her Welsh grandfather. Tasha, like poor Jennifer, had woken up one morning and, as if from heaven, had had the wildness dropped upon her. She had the wild eyes of her mother, and suddenly liked music, short skirts, and boys.

Mrs Barcroft hoped her granddaughter would be well, hoped she would snap out of it, and wouldn't replicate her mother's mistakes.

Jennifer had run away to Manchester at seventeen. The next time she saw her, Jennifer was dropping off baby Tasha.

She couldn't handle it anymore, she'd said. *Don't be too cruel to her*, she said, and then left.

What Jennifer never understood, was that cruelty was necessary.

Mrs Barcroft crossed to the other side of her office and looked down at the courtyard below. There, kicking a path through the snow, came the Inspector.

She hadn't met this Inspector yet. He was new to the local force and had no doubt been too busy with the snow and ice to visit the school. He came now though, and the hunch in his posture, the linger in his step, and the fact that the walk had taken him seven minutes already, told her that he bore bad news.

She was prepared for it. Children die in cold winters. She'd been there for the deep drifts in the seventies. The big freeze of 2010 seemed like only yesterday. The Avon Murray School had lost pupils in both.

No doubt, Mrs Barcroft sighed, we have lost some again.

Always, always children must place themselves in danger. Never do they learn that danger has a price. Still, she reconciled herself, it was always the naughty ones who get caught. Always the ones who push too far. The ones without any sense of the rules, or without any sense whatsoever.

Inspector Todor knocked on the buffed chipboard. Mrs Barcroft's door held firm.

For a moment, she ignored him.

The snow began to fall again. Only a small sprinkling now. The school had been open for two days. They had opened when no one else would. The rest of the town was still frozen solid.

But Mrs Barcroft had insisted, and she'd been right. Even now, a small and despondent group of children were roving from class to near-empty class, learning from whatever teachers they could find. Very few had braved the storm, but they were there. Learning.

Yesterday there had been almost no one. Today there were more. Tomorrow, she felt sure, there would be more and yet more again. Discipline would overcome. Discipline would restore routine.

The knock came again.

She swallowed and straightened her cardigan.

'Come in.'

The door opened and Todor stepped in. He wore a long coat, trailed in mud, and his knees were wet from snow.

His first act was to take out his identification card and pass it to Mrs Barcroft.

'Inspector Dafydd Todor,' she read aloud. 'So, you're Welsh?'

The Inspector nodded. Curiously mute.

'My husband was Welsh,' Mrs Barcroft said, returning the card.

'What happened to him?' Todor asked.

He'd picked up on the past tense.

Mrs Barcroft looked at the Inspector, her eyes narrowing, head tilting. She shook her head as she spoke.

'Why, he's dead of course.'

The Inspector put his hands in his pockets.

'I'm sorry to hear that, ma'am.'

'It was thirty-five years ago.'

Mrs Barcroft pursed her lips.

'I'm no longer in mourning, Inspector Todor. You don't have to offer your condolences.'

The Inspector nodded. He noticed his hands were in

his pockets and he swiftly pulled them out.

'Would you care to take a seat, Inspector Todor?'

The Inspector looked at the hard-plastic chair and shook his head.

'I'd rather stand, Mrs Barcroft, if that's alright with you?'

'Quite alright.'

She turned to look out the window. 'I prefer to stand myself.'

Chapter Five

Inspector Todor

Todor's hands had somehow returned to his pockets. He pulled them out again and held them behind his back.

He was uncertain how to stand in situations like this one. There hadn't been any training. How should one stand when about to deliver the worst news imaginable?

The Inspector knew the headmistress already, he felt. He'd heard so much about her. *A fire breathing dragon,* they'd laughed at the station; *perfect for a Taff like you,* eh? The joke didn't seem so funny now that he was in her office, faced by the stacks of papers and the annuals and ledgers, the pictures of past years and somewhere, he was sure, a picture of her granddaughter.

He knew Mrs Barcroft was legally responsible for her granddaughter, but he didn't know why. The Inspector felt woefully underprepared for the task at hand.

'Let me guess,' Mrs Barcroft said, staring out at the falling snow. 'You are about to tell me some bad news-'

The Inspector swallowed.

'-Yes, Mrs Barcroft.'

'I hadn't finished, Inspector'.

She cut him off, holding the silence for a moment.

From down below came the sound of shouting, leaking from one of the classrooms. It was muffled by the condensation dripping down the windows, and blown about on the icy wind. Strange and hollow sounds, but they had reached her.

'I would predict,' Mrs Barcroft continued. 'That the news is of the terrible kind that cannot be broken directly. I expect that it is a terrible thing that has happened. I expect that it means the death of a child.'

The Inspector began to tremble.

'How… How did you know?'

Mrs Barcroft turned to face him. Her eyes were dazzling blue.

I've been around a long time, Inspector. I know how things work around here. What is shocking to you has, sadly, become an all too common occurrence at this school. It is one with which I'm familiar. Time, after all, teaches us many lessons. Often ones we would've preferred not to learn.

'So, tell me, what is the name of the pupil? Or is it pupils? Who has the winter claimed this year?'

'Why,' Inspector Todor's lip shook. 'It's Tasha. Your granddaughter. Tasha Barcroft.'

Mrs Barcroft gasped.

Feeling her face suddenly flush, she span around quickly, reaching for the windowsill and the nearest handhold. She put a hand to the glass, closed her eyes, and ran her fingers along the frozen pane. She fought to appear calm, to appear controlled.

The snow kept falling. It fell in slow and lazy flakes. A tear threatened to roll down her cheek.

'I'm very sorry, Mrs Barcroft,' Inspector Todor began. 'Her death is a true tragedy.'

'Where?' the headteacher asked, her voice refusing to wobble. 'Where did you find her?'

Inspector Todor lifted out his notebook and thumbed through the pages. He'd not been able to ascertain the name of the river yet.

'She's in a river,' he mumbled. 'Frozen beneath the ice.'

'Which river?'

Mrs Barcroft rubbed her eyes. Then, with a sharp intake of breath, turned to him. The Inspector saw her eyes were puffy and red.

'*Is* frozen? *Is*? You mean you haven't got her out yet?'

'The river is considered a crime scene,' the Inspector began.

He'd prepared this line in the car, but as he spoke he heard its hollowness.

'We tried to get her out already. It didn't work. Two officers are in the hospital after falling in themselves. The valley is too steep for special equipment. The tree cover is too thick for a helicopter. Then, of course, there's the snow storm...'

'Enough,' Mrs Barcroft snapped. 'Enough excuses.'

She walked to her desk. She lifted a picture frame. As the Inspector watched, she carried it over to the window. She placed it face-down on the sill, leaning on the photo as she looked out at the snow.

'So,' Mrs Barcroft swallowed. 'How do you think she came to be in the water?'

She watched as Lucas, a snowball striking the back of his head, turned around and pushed a young girl over. She fell, screaming and laughing, back into a pile of powder.

'Murder,' Inspector Todor said.

For the second time, her eyes opened wide.

'Murder?'

The Inspector nodded. He was leafing now, non-committally, through his notebook. He blinked down at a page, eyes passing vaguely over its surface before he flicked to another. Perhaps he should've told her it was a murder straight away? *Or would the shock have been too much?* She thought.

'So?'

Mrs Barcroft lifted her hands up. She looked like she was pleading, but there was anger in her eyes.

'Are you going to tell me any more than this? Or only that my granddaughter has been murdered, and you cannot retrieve her body?'

'Erm,' the Inspector ran a finger through his notebook.

'Well the body was found by a local man who was out walking his dog. From what we could see, she had been, *has* been, frozen solid for quite a while now. Her body is in a remarkable state of preservation-'

'Remarkable?'

'Yes. There are no visible marks of struggle anywhere. From what we can see, it was the ice that killed her.'

Mrs Barcroft turned around. She placed both hands on her desk, steadying herself.

'Well,' she swallowed. 'On with it!'

The Inspector flipped a page and continued.

'The witness, the man walking his dog, reported he saw a strange looking man out in the woods. The description of the suspect matched a young man named Todd Morrow; he's a local forest ranger and a bit of a recluse; by all accounts a strange man. We have him in custody.'

'Why?'

'Why, Mrs Barcroft?' the Inspector paused. 'Why, he's suspected of murder. The murder of your granddaughter. That's why we have him in custody.'

'I know *that*!'

She startled him, her piercing eyes sending a shudder right through his body.

'I was asking, Inspector, why would he do it? Why would he murder her?'

The Inspector thought for a moment.

'To be plain with you, Mrs Barcroft, it is not a matter of "*why*" at the current moment. So far, all we know is that Todd Morrow was seen watching the body. When approached by Mr Farringdon-'

'Mr Farringdon?'

'The witness, yes, Mr William Farringdon.'

Her eyes darted to the window again.

'When the witness approached Mr Morrow, the forest ranger proceeded to flee from him. He was visibly panicked and, when our officers finally caught up with him, he resisted arrest. He came at one of them with a pocket knife, in fact, but he was soon subdued.

'In short, we have every reason to suspect he is the criminal in question. He was found at the crime scene, with a weapon, and when approached by members of law enforcement, he proceeded to flee.

'I can confirm too, Mrs Barcroft, that he has not denied the charges.'

The headteacher swallowed. Her throat was so dry.

She was staring at Lucas Farringdon. *The boy's father had found the body, had he?* And there the boy was now, returned to school, blissfully unaware, unbothered by the death.

'So,' Mrs Barcroft mumbled. 'Todd Morrow's admitted it?'

'Not as such,' the Inspector said. 'He's simply refusing to talk. He won't say anything either way. I've seen murderers do similar. Particularly ones who have acted without reason, without logic or spite, but purely as animals. Those kinds of men don't talk. Their actions are beyond language, and so they tend to be silent.'

'That doesn't tell us why,' Mrs Barcroft replied. 'It tells us nothing. You're not the only one who knows human behaviour, Inspector.'

Perhaps feeling he'd said his part, the Inspector remained silent.

'You know, I could bring any one of these boys up here and charge them with invented crimes; crimes they've had no part in, perhaps have never even heard of. Most, Inspector, will stay entirely silent. It's only later, once the magnitude of the unfairness has settled in, that they will think to respond.

'The guilty boy, Inspector Todor, is the opposite. He will protest his innocence before a single charge is even raised. You won't be able to shut a guilty boy up, Inspector.

'That is my experience with boys. They're always the same. Never changing in over forty years of teaching them. And you tell me that poor Todd Morrow won't deny the charges?'

She turned away from the Inspector for the last time.

What she said now would be her final word. He'd said his piece and clearly wanted to do was leave, as if he'd done his duty and conveyed the information.

'I taught Todd Morrow,' she said. 'He was a good boy. A popular boy. I don't know what happened to him when he left for the city, but he came back changed, didn't like people anymore. I can't say I blame him. So, he went to live in the woods.

'I doubt the boy's spoken to another human being for over a year. Of course, he ran away, and of course he won't talk. That is how Todd Morrow is, Inspector. So, don't be so quick to rush to judgements.'

Inspector Todor bowed and thanked her for her advice. He gave, once again, his condolences, before backing out the door. It closed with a creak.

She'd hidden her emotions from the Inspector. Now, standing alone in her office, she hid her emotions from herself.

She ran a handkerchief along her cheek and dabbed it under her eyes.

Somewhere beneath a series of bells rang for lunchtime.

Children spilled out over the playing fields. They ranged from the very small, thirteen-year-olds still sucking their sleeves, to the sixteen-year-olds, some already six-foot tall.

Boys and girls. All curiously alike in their woollen trousers and baggy coats. And down there, among them, was Lucas Farringdon. She watched from her high window, she saw her granddaughter's young boyfriend, striding out across the snowdrifts with his friends, laughing.

Chapter Six

Lucas Farringdon

He'd arrived late in the morning, escaping as his father walked the dog.

'It's messed up what two weeks inside can do to you!'

He laughed as he walked out of class, legs soaked with meltwater.

'Never thought I'd be desperate to come back here!'

He walked with his friends, pushing each other over and piling snow over the fallen. They trudged out into the snow, coats dripping, their laughter rising high on the winter wind.

'So, you guys haven't seen Tasha anywhere?'

'Fuck off Luke-*arse*,' Tegan laughed. 'You just want to bum her.'

Lucas hit her in the face with another snowball.

'I'm not saying anything, Teeg. I'm just wondering where she's been. She's not been on her phone for ages.'

Mike shrugged. Jace spoke through a bruised lip.

'Maybe she's found another guy, mate.'

'Another guy?' Lucas laughed, shoving. 'In a snowstorm? I was lucky to even get out this morning. Had to sneak out when Dad was off with the dog. What's Tasha gonna do? Ride a dog sled about, hunting for dick like an Eskimo?'

The others cracked up laughing. They all looked up to Lucas. He was the only one of them to have a girlfriend; the only one to have *done it*. And he was so cool about it. None of the sullenness that the bully kids had about their possibly made-up girlfriends. No, Lucas was cool, and everyone knew it.

'So, the Dragon's been in this whole time?' he said, looking up at the headteacher's window. 'But no sign of Tasha?'

'Seems so, chief,' Jace nodded. Mike shrugged.

'That's weird.'

Lucas scratched at his wet knee.

As they stepped out of the snow and into the lunch room, he felt a buzzing in his trouser pocket. He took out his phone. A missed call from his home number.

It was his father, ringing him.

Lucas Farringdon stared for a moment at the lit-up screen. Then, telling his friends that he'd catch up with them, he accepted the call.

'Dad?'

* * *

Lucas flung his bag down, peeled off his sodden outer coat and took off his jumper that, despite his coat, was soaked through, only to find that the shirt beneath was also wet.

He stripped down to thermals in the empty kitchen.

Scout barked softly from her bed.

'Dad!' he shouted. 'I'm back!'

He knew his father must be around somewhere. If his dad had called him home it must've been something urgent. For his dad to even think of using the phone meant some kind of emergency. Normally Farringdon senior never touched them.

Chapter Seven

William Farringdon

He'd called his son after an hour spent ruminating in the study. He was lurking there when he heard Lucas' voice.

'Coming, Lucas!' he called. 'Just a second.'

Despite the half-formed thoughts that swam in his head, he'd yet to work out how he would tell his son. He'd imagined the start of the conversation a hundred, perhaps a thousand times. Each time he found himself thinking of something else.

Thinking of the news coverage; of his daughter, Jo, away at university; of the body, frozen beneath the ice.

Lucas had shed his wet things and pulled on new ones. Warm and fresh from the dryer. As he walked into the living room he ran into his father coming the other way.

'Sorry, Lucas.'

The two stepped back from each other. They couldn't look each other in the eye. Instead, they stood there, transfixed by the situation.

William turned red.

'It's Tasha, son,' he mumbled. 'Have you heard?'

'Heard?' Lucas asked, his eyes widening. 'Has something

happened? She wasn't in school today. I thought it was strange because Mrs Barcroft has been in for two days now...'

'She's dead,' William said.

'What?'

'She's dead, Lucas. I'm sorry, but she's dead.'

Lucas looked at this father, and his father back at him. With a slow inevitability, tears welled up in Lucas' eyes. They were both breathing heavy.

'But,' Lucas began. 'But... how? What happened?'

'Murder, they think.'

William's fingers drifted up to his moustache. He spoke through his hand. Each word hurt, but he knew he had to say it. Better a short, sharp shock.

'That recluse, Todd Morrow. I found the body and I saw him looking at it. He ran away and the police think it's him. It's hard to think about, but she's frozen now. Fallen in the river and frozen.'

'Which river?' Lucas mumbled like he was half-asleep. Still in shock.

'The one where I walk Scout, I suppose. Tasha's in the pool by the footbridge. You know, where we go swimming sometimes in the summer.'

Hearing her name, Scout barked from the other room.

Lucas buried his head in his hands. He began to cry. Sobbing, and wept heavily. His hand reaching out for sofa and a firm seat.

William stood and watched his son.

He knew he should comfort him. Yet, somehow, he

couldn't move, fixed in place, arms locked rigid to his side. He stood there, looking, a gulf between them. Lucas was gasping between sobs.

Then, between sharp intakes of breath, he cried out.

'That was where we had our first date!'

William's face flushed redder. He'd known his son and the Barcroft girl were courting, but he'd never thought of them as dates. It all seemed so grown up. And Lucas was his youngest.

'Now, now.'

Feebly, Lucas reached out and embraced his father around the middle. William found himself stroking his son's hair.

As his son held on to him, William felt a sense of foreboding.

He'd known very little about his son's girlfriend. She was, to his knowledge, Lucas' first. If it wasn't for this... total *aberration*, then this first love, like all of them, would have soon passed.

Wasn't this part of the reason for escaping to the country? Morals were supposed to be freer out there. He'd grown up in the country and had his string of girlfriends too. The first break up stung, yes, but there were many more girls in the valley – or, if not in the valley, then a valley over. It had been the same with his daughter, Jo. The forests and the fields made you free. They made life free. That was the idea.

His wife, Helen, was a city girl. She'd internalised the overcrowding. Ten thousand eyes watched her at all times.

Even in her dark bedroom, the covers over her head.

It wasn't inaccurate to say that William had moved the family out to Avon Murray in order that his children might grow up differently to his wife. But now this…

William wondered if this death would ruin his son forever. Stroking his hair, he felt the thoughts in the lad's head turning over and over. His little skull was like a shaken coconut. The memories swirled around, getting sweeter and sweeter. The tatty little schoolgirl, his first fling, was now doomed to haunt him forever.

'I loved her, dad.' Lucas whispered. 'I know you don't believe me, but I did.'

'I know, son.'

William patted the boy's back.

'You don't have to tell me.'

'I just…'

Lucas broke away from his father and lay back on the sofa.

'I just don't know what I'm going to do.'

William looked down at his son and was lost again. How should you deal with another's sorrow, when you're so filled with a different type of pain?

William promptly left the room.

Chapter Eight

Lucas Farringdon

Time passed. From the doorway came tinkling.

'Alright.'

William returned with two crystal glasses both containing an amber liquid, his finest scotch.

His father saved it under lock and key, away from his mother's thirsty fingers. It was meant for special occasions. This may not have been special, in the   traditional sense, but it was certainly an occasion.

'Alright, drink!'

William handed his son the glass.

Lucas sat up.

William swirled the whisky around the glass, rolling air into it. Lucas mimicked him. Then, seeing his   father neck the mixture in one gulp, Lucas tried it too, but choked and sputtered.

'It's alright, son,' William nodded. 'It takes some getting used to. It should calm your nerves, regardless.'

As he stopped coughing he felt his throat, once burning, now turn numb. His head tingled.

Seconds later, he felt giddy. His love seemed to soar

up above him on golden wings. He realised that now, crystallised in death, her love for him would last forever.

Then the feeling faded. He felt silly for feeling it. He felt guilty.

'I know it's not an optimal solution,' William said, rattling his ice.

'Is this how mum feels?' Lucas asked.

He lowered himself back down onto the sofa.

William looked down on his son and was silent.

He hadn't intended to draw such direct parallels with his mother. Nevertheless, there they were. The initiation of another family drunk.

'Don't worry about your mother, Lucas,' William said. 'You have your own problems now. Life has thrown you into its seriousness too early for my liking, but here you are. The older one gets the less one must suffer on behalf of others. You must suffer for yourself now.'

'For myself? But what about Tasha? What about her family? Mrs Barcroft?'

'There'll be time enough for that, son,' William patted the boy's head again. 'You must bear your own burdens first.'

Lucas turned over, away from his father.

'All things pass, son. Let me tell you that now. All that you have will one day either pass away, or change. Some things change so much that you will wish they *had* passed. It's a gentleman's job to learn renunciation.

'In this life, nobody will thank you, the best will pass faster than the worst, and nothing will ever make sense until it is all far behind you. The world has a bitter taste,

Lucas. And yet, you have to savour it.' William's work was done. But he couldn't help himself, could he? He kept talking Until his words turned bitter and whisky-darkened.

'Okay, dad.'

Lucas' head was buried in a pile of cushions, trying to sleep.

William nodded and turned away, only to turn back, at the prompting of the whisky, and add his last thoughts. He scrubbed roughly at his moustache as he spoke.

'You should remember these feelings, boy. You'll never feel as strongly as you do now. Not about anything. Neither good nor bad. You should remember that.'

'Remember what?'

The two men froze. The voice had come from the hallway door.

Lucas unburied his head and turned in the direction of the voice.

It was his mother.

Helen Farringdon stood at the door in her grey pyjamas. The pale light of the winter washed in from a window behind her. She made a ghostly silhouette, standing there.

'What are you remembering?'

Her eyes were on the two empty glasses, cut crystal, resting on the dark wood of the coffee table.

'Nothing, Helen,' William said. 'It's something to do with Lucas. He's having a very stressful time. I can come and explain it to you later.'

Helen looked up at her husband and down at her son.

'Are you celebrating?'

'No, Helen.'

William shook his head. He took a step towards her but, as he did, the panicked look in her eye stopped him.

His mother took a step into the room and stared at Lucas. Her voice was frail and delicate, worn out by strong spirits.

'Are you sure you're not celebrating, Lucas?'

She took another step into the room.

'Have I missed your birthday?'

'It's not his birthday,' William said.

'Then what is it?'

Her hands started to tremble. She'd lifted them up, like a sleepwalker.

'What else have I forgotten? What else have I missed?'

'You've missed nothing,' William said curtly. 'This is something else, Helen. I'll speak to you about it later'.

Her trembling stopped. She stopped advancing. Lucas had buried his head again. He was hidden from her. In one sudden movement, she balled her hand into a fist and jabbed a finger at William.

'What are you hiding from me?'

It was as much an accusation as a question.

'We are hiding nothing, dear…'

'Don't call me that!' she yelled now.

Her voice was growing in power. Her eyes were turning wild.

It was the face of a woman who had demanded to be seen and then, upon being seen by everyone, had remembered that all she'd ever wanted was to hide.

'You get to bed, darling.'

He spoke calmly, bent at the neck, making himself small.

'You get to bed and I'll bring some of this up, yes?' He pointed to the empty glasses.

'I'll explain it all then.'

Helen looked down at the glasses and then up at William. Her eyes turned to Lucas, who was peering out from beneath a cushion. Seeing she was watched, Helen pulled herself up, tall and prideful, swaying a little in the cold light. Her grief-stricken features hardened to a snarl.

'Is this what you think of me?' she asked William.

William looked down at the glasses and then up at her. He couldn't answer.

She'd heard him at his private liquor cabinet. This is what had brought her down, they realised.

'I came down out of love.'

Helen was on the verge of angry tears now.

'I came down here out of concern.'

'I'm sorry, dear.'

'Don't call me that!' she screamed. 'Don't think you can buy me off with your drink! Is that all you think I am?'

At that moment, the doorbell rang.

The three were silent. They looked around, each to each, and then all three at the hallway door. The ringing had come from the kitchen. Friends, what few the Farringdons had, used the door at the back.

The bell rang again.

William looked down at his son. The boy's face was grey, as grey as his mother's pyjamas in the afternoon light. He looked back at Helen. Her face showed no signs of its former rage. Only anxiety was there now. She would have fled, no doubt, back to her bedroom, if the suddenness of the sound hadn't bolted her in place.

Lucas trusted they wouldn't do anything stupid, at least not suddenly. His father strode off to the kitchen door.

Chapter Nine

William Farringdon

'Hold on!' William shouted 'I'm coming!'

At the doorway was a crumpled figure. He was turned away, watching the snow. William could see nothing of the man but his wet and dirty overcoat. The dark curls that clung to his head.

'Can I help you?'

As the figure turned he recognised the Inspector. He looked different from this morning. His face was bleak.

'Hello Mr Farringdon, I'm afraid it's bad news. Might I come in?'

William nodded and stepped aside.

In the living room, Lucas was still buried beneath the cushions.

His ears pricked up, listening for his father's voice. His mother hung in the doorway, swaying like a spirit.

Inspector Todor was apologising to William over and over as he entered the living room.

'Really, I truly am sorry for this. It goes against all my better instincts. I'm very sorry.'

William stepped into the living room with the Inspector

at his heel.

'This is Inspector Dafydd Todor,' he announced. 'He is the officer leading the investigation into Tasha's murder. I met him this morning.'

William spoke directly to Helen. Her eyes bulged wide as they darted between William, the Inspector and her cowering son.

'He seems like a good man,' William said, turning to his son. 'Everything will be alright, Lucas.'

'What?'

Lucas rose white from his hiding place.

'I'm sorry, Lucas,' the Inspector said, rubbing his hands together.

He looked the very model of regret as he lifted his handcuffs from his pocket

'I'm arresting you, Lucas, you see. I'm arresting you on the suspicion of murder; the murder of Tasha Barcroft. You have the right to remain silent, and,' he trembled as the boy started to cry. 'And I'd like you to come with me to answer a few questions. It'll just be a few questions, Lucas. I'd like you to come in without a fuss.'

Lucas, tears rolling down his cheeks, turned to his father. William, his upper lip stiff, nodded to his son. He kept his eye on the Welsh Inspector. The policeman stood a half-foot shorter than William, and his cowering emphasised the difference yet further.

'It'll be okay,' William nodded. 'You go with him, son. I'll come along too. I'll be following in the car, right behind you the whole time. I'll be outside of the room when they're questioning you. I'll be right there, Lucas. You have nothing to worry about.'

Todor inhaled as if preparing to correct the older man, but thought better of it. Instead, he watched as the boy stood and offered his wrists.

'I'm ready,' Lucas said. 'I'll come with you.'

'Good lad.'

The Inspector Todor relaced the cuffs in his jacket pocket and led the boy away by the arm.

'You're a good lad, Lucas.'

William began to follow.

Then, as they were leaving the room, a cry echoed through the air after them. Helen, tearing at her hair, cried out.

'Murderer! Murderer! My son! My own boy is a murderer!'

William saw the madness in her eyes. He saw the way she rolled around, drunk on the verge of oblivion. He should help her, he knew, but his son was already being led away.

'You!'

Helen screamed at William. She leaned now against the doorframe, her finger once again pointing.

'You helped him! I saw it! You're a murderer too! Worse than a murderer! You're all murderers!'

William turned his back on her and marched out after his son.

Helen, her family gone, left alone, sank down against the doorframe. She would weep there until her throat grew dry, and then she would attend to the unlocked cabinet.

Chapter Ten

Frigg McBride

The few children who had made it into school on that second snowless day were rounded up and taken to the main assembly hall. They sat cross-legged in rows while the headteacher, the rarely seen Mrs Barcroft, prepared to speak.

The perceptive children noted the pallor of her features and the steepness of her stoop. She walked very slowly to the front of the hall.

'Boys and girls,' Mrs Barcroft announced. 'Today a terrible thing has happened. A pupil who was once with us has now gone. Gone forever. The terrible storm that closed the school has, I am very sorry to announce, taken a life.'

The hall was filled with whispers. The children rocked from side to side; some chirruping with their friends, others fidgeting, mouths agape, guessing who it was.

'Tasha Barcroft was a good girl-' Mrs Barcroft began, only to catch herself mid-sob.

The girls in Tasha's year made an audible intake of breath. Some of the older boys muttered expletives. There were even some awkward giggles.

The younger children didn't know what to do and so

simply sat, open mouthed.

'Tasha, as you may know, was my granddaughter.'

Mrs Barcroft removed a handkerchief from her pocket and dabbed at her eye.

'She was my granddaughter, but she was a friend to all of us. She was a good girl, and her loss is a tragedy. We will miss her, always. All of us.'

In the lower years a child started crying. It was enough to inspire others, and soon the whole of the lower school broke out into wailing.

'That is why,' Mrs Barcroft continued, projecting her voice. 'I am declaring the rest of the day to be a school holiday. You are welcome to stay and attend the normal afterschool activities, but there will be no more lessons. Our school is in shock. It is now time to grieve.'

Mrs Barcroft turned and strode out of the hall. The little children wailed on for a moment and then, as normal, the hall erupted into a hundred tiny conversations.

'No way!' Erin said, turning back to stare at Frigg. 'I can't believe the bitch is dead!'

Frigite McBride, Frigg to her friends, rolled her eyes.

Erin turned to the portly girl sat beside her.

'Mary. Let's get out of here, yeah?'

Mary nodded.

'Coming Frigg?'

Frigg lifted her compact from her bag and checked her eyeliner. Finding it still thickly applied and unrun, she clicked the compact closed and stood up, slinging her bag over her shoulder.

She followed the two girls out of the hall, joining the crush of bodies all funnelling through the exit.

The children poured out of the school like spilled milk. The snow, settled whitely on the ground, was rapidly stamped to brown. Row upon row of dancing, shuffling, running, jumping and dragging feet spread out along the pavements.

Only as their paths grew wider apart did the children begin to regain their individual characteristics. The flood of blue-blazered youth lapped at doorways and splashed against bus stops. They trickled away down side streets and, after a few quick phone calls, climbed dripping into Land Rovers. The parents soon filled the roads, as the children did the streets. Exhausts sputtered in the cold air.

'So, what do you think she died of?' Mary asked her friends.

The three walked together along the main road. They all lived up near the church, on the other side of town, with Frigg living further out than any of them. Frigg was a Goth, and Erin and Mary were in awe of that.

'Who cares,' Erin frowned. 'If you ask me she got what she deserved. She was such a bitch.'

'She was a bully,' Mary agreed.

Frigg sighed. She'd been bullied by Tasha worse than either of them. In fact, she doubted if Tasha even knew who Mary and Erin were. They hated Tasha because of how Tasha treated Frigg. They were angry on her behalf which, Frigg realised, made them angrier than she was. Or at least that's how it appeared.

'Maybe one of the people she bullied finally caught up with her?' Erin said. 'Maybe it was *murder*!'

Mary laughed, a warm and endearing laugh. Not the kind one associates with murder.

Frigg sighed again.

'What's up, Frigg?' Mary said, prodding her arm. 'Are you not glad she's gone?'

Frigg looked down at her Doc Martins as they kicked hopelessly through the snow.

'I'm not sure.'

She wasn't sure of anything. She'd felt that a lot lately; a total and utter indifference to the world's woes, and to her own. She was unpopular, perhaps. Teased. That didn't move her. And now, it seemed, neither did death.

She remembered Tasha and her cronies holding her down and burning her with tapers in science class. *Burn the witch*, they'd chanted. When Tasha, with her angry, spiteful eyes, couldn't get Frigg's clothes alight she instead went to the sink and filled a cup with water. She threw it over Frigg's head.

'You can't burn witches,' she spat. 'You have to drown them.'

Then her cronies had kicked at Frigg and pulled her hair.

Despite all the will she had telling her not to, Frigg started to cry.

'Look!' Tasha had laughed. 'She's melting! She's melting!'

All that came back to Frigg now like a scene from an aquarium. Tasha thrashed around in her memory like a colourful fish. Even her past self, white skin and thick black eyeliner, resembled to her now an exotic undersea animal.

The scene was something separate from her. It was the past. She couldn't even tap on the glass.

'Maybe it was what her mum died of?' Erin wondered.

Mary corrected her. 'Her mum's not dead, Erin.'

'Why does she live with her grandma then?'

Mary shrugged.

'I don't know. Maybe her mum's in a different country or something? My dad goes away on business sometimes. We stay with granddad then.'

'Well if Tasha's mum goes away on business then she goes away *a lot*,' Erin laughed. 'She's probably a prostitute.'

'Erin!' Mary laughed her wholesome laugh, turning red.

'Maybe she killed herself.' Frigg said coldly without any emotion. The other two were silent. They walked for a little while in silence. Frigg was vaguely aware of having upset them, but walked on regardless. She was inside of her fishbowl now. The glass had descended, separating her from her friends, and from the world around her.

Somewhere, someone's phone buzzed.

Mary and Erin patted their jacket pockets. Frigg opened her bag and felt around inside.

'Oh, it's me!'

Mary smiled. She pulled the vibrating plastic from her pocket and gazed deep into the screen.

'So,' Erin asked. 'What is it?

'It...'

Mary stuttered, stumbling over her words. It was impossible to tell if it was good excitement or bad.

Frigg looked at her friend with wide, mascara-punctuated eyes. From feeling nothing, her stomach had just sank.

'It *was* a murder,' Mary said rapidly. 'It was, it was!'

'Tasha?' Erin asked.

'Yes!' Mary replied, running now and grabbing Frigg. 'Katy Hanneton said so! She's texted everyone. Her dad saw Lucas Farringdon being driven in the back of a police car. They say that he did it! That he's been arrested!'

Frigg felt sick.

'Lucas?' Erin blinked. 'But, he can't have! I know he was going out with Tasha and stuff but... he was *nice*, wasn't he?'

Mary shook her head.

'You can't tell. My mum always says you can't tell with boys. The good ones are sometimes the most evil.'

Frigg didn't hear the rest of their conversation. She walked on with her eyes on the snowdrifts. Yes, she'd been indifferent to Tasha. Perhaps she'd thought her cruel and malicious, but only as you could find a cat malicious. Cruelty was in Tasha's nature. But Lucas?

She'd been lab partners with Lucas. Last year in fact. He was an upbeat boy. He had blonde hair and when his fringe fell over his eyes he shook it back like a dog.

He was a lot like a puppy actually. He was endearing, loving almost... but you knew that the second he stopped looking at you he'd have forgotten you. He'd already be on to the next thing.

She remembered the ritual.

Frigg held her breath. Of all the things to remember, she couldn't believe she'd remembered that.

'-didn't you Frigg?'

Frigg blinked. Erin was talking to her. Erin peered with those almond-shaped eyes of hers, probing Frigg's reaction.

Frigg wasn't listening. 'What?' she asked.

'I said you had him in chemistry, didn't you? Lucas Farringdon.'

Frigg nodded.

'Well, there you go. It could just as easily have been *her*!'

Erin nodded sagely. Mary nodded too.

Mary began reciting something she'd heard in a podcast about serial killers.

'You know, that's how psychopaths are. They look all friendly, but then inside they don't think like we do. They don't have any empathy. They call it superficial charm.'

'Like a magic charm?' Erin asked. 'Or like a Prince Charming charm?'

Frigg saw the turning up ahead. It was the one that sent the two girls left and herself right. They lived in narrow terraces typical of Avon Murray, redbrick with small square gardens behind them. Frigg didn't. She and her mum and her cat Merlin all huddled together in a bungalow just down from the church.

Her mum said the cottage was older than everything else in the town. She said that when the cottage was first

71

built, it had all been fields. Frigg didn't believe her.

'So,' Frigg said. 'Where did you say the murder was?'

Mary switched off her monologue in mid-flow like a tap.

'Well,' Erin said, gazing at her phone. 'According to some people on Facebook – get this – they've not even moved the body yet! He killed her by the bridge down the valley. You know - the pool where we go swimming? Down from the high woods but before the millpond.'

Frigg nodded. She knew the pool well.

Mary gasped. 'You're not thinking of going are you, Frigg?'

'There's one police lady there, they say, but that's it. The rest who went down all came back up. Two of them even got picked up by an ambulance.'

'An ambulance?'

'Oh my God!' Mary whispered. 'He must have attacked the policemen too!'

'They might have been police ladies,' Erin said, a knowing smirk crossing her purple-glossed lips.

'Police officers,' Frigg corrected.

She hated herself for that. She'd said she would stop correcting people.

'Technically,' she said. 'That's what they're technically called, I think.'

Erin looked disappointed at having been caught out. Mary carried on regardless. 'They say that murders can be sexual. Like it gives the murderers a thrill to kill ladies.'

'Nasty,' Erin shrugged. 'Oh well, I hope you're alright, Frigg. You liked him, didn't you?'

'Oh no!' Mary held her fingers to her lips. 'You were

in love with a murderer!'

Frigg ignored them and, stopping at the corner, gave them their daily hugs and waved them away down the street. The redbrick terrace glowed in the snow like the breast of a robin. The snow piled up on windowsills and on top of recycling bins. As they walked away, a cold wind seemed to carry them off.

Frigg turned in the direction of home and began to walk. Yet, the further she walked, the less she felt the draw of home. There wasn't much warmth there in the winter. The house was too old for central heating, her mother said, which meant sitting by the fire with blanket after blanket piled up on top of you. It was colder inside than out sometimes. She didn't feel like going back just yet.

Instead, she felt another draw. It was the call of the river. The frozen river with the body in it.

She knew it was a foolish thought. A mad one, perhaps. But she needed to see the body. Something inside her needed to.

She, after all, may have caused it.

Frigg pulled her black hoody close around her and reached in her bag for a scarf. Her fingerless gloves were wet with snow but warmer than going bare-handed.

When she reached the roundabout by the butchers, she had to make a choice. Did she turn up the hill to the church and go home? Or did she walk on, to the river? Without thinking, she walked on.

Strange feelings. Disconnection and, at the same time,

guilt. Hard to imagine the two together, the one never cancelling the other, but there they were. It was as if the guilty party sat inside, driving her disconnected body onwards. It drove her towards the river.

It had been fourteen months now. Fourteen or fifteen. It was last school year and she'd been lab partners with Lucas Farringdon.

'Luke', she'd called him then. That wasn't his real name, she knew. He was Lucas, and everyone called him Lucas but, to her, that year, he'd been Luke. Or, sometimes, Luca. Her own special name for him. One that nobody else would ever use.

They scorched magnesium together. They rolled mercury around in test tubes. He added too much vinegar to baking soda and it ran out all over their hands. His fringe flopped down and she stuck it back up with the bubbles. He smiled.

She didn't think Lucas was a murderer. But she might be.

When he told her about his new girlfriend, he spoke as if Frigg didn't know who she was. As if he hadn't noticed that Tasha Barcroft, the love of his life apparently, had always sought out Frigg as a punching bag. Tasha Barcroft? It was too much to believe.

And so, she had to do it. She loved Lucas Farringdon. She thought of her name: Frigite Farringdon. It almost sounded okay. But now Tasha was going to take that away from her, the same way she used to take her lunch money.

She cried back then. Those nights full of feelings. Merlin had crawled up on her bed with her. He was black all over, but for a little James Bond tuxedo of white on his upper chest. His tail wafted like a magic wand.

He crawled up on her bed and then into her arms. He soaked up her silly tears. He made her feel not so silly anymore.

He gave her inspiration.

Of course, the murder had happened in the woods. Of course. Because that's where the ritual happened.

She'd taken two buses and gone all the way to Manchester to find the right spell. She'd found it in a Northern Quarter shop where she liked to buy jewellery. They specialised in Goth accessories, heavy metal CDs and esoteric items. They had a number of spell books. Frigg had seen them before. But only one had the spell she wanted.

Love. A spell that drove a boy mad. A spell that made him do anything for your love. He would fail his studies. He would abandon his friends. He would kill his lover…

In chemistry, she'd tricked him into giving her his hair. The beautiful blonde fringe that sat up there, taunting her; falling, with increasing regularity, around his soft eyes.

She'd pulled a strand of her own hair out and told him about how disgusting the smell of burning hair was. He'd laughed and sniffed as she put her single strand to the Bunsen burner.

'I can't smell anything,' he said.

'Maybe you need more hair,' she replied.

'Well cut more off!'

'I'm not cutting anything off,' she said. 'Why don't you?'

'Okay. 'Get some scissors.'

The hair did smell bad, once you had enough of it. But, more importantly, Frigg had pocketed some of his golden strands.

As she carried them home she felt excited, sexually. It was a powerful feeling. A feeling to drive you mad. The spell·required his hair or his nail clippings, and to mix it with her menses.

She'd done it in the woods. The woods that she stepped into now. She'd done it on the banks of the river; flowing then, now frozen. She walked along the same path towards the site of the murder. She would pass the place of the ritual as she approached the body.

It was a cloudless night with a full moon.

She carried Merlin with her. His yellow eyes beamed out of the dark, keeping her safe.

She'd traced a circle in the ground, carving it with the side of her Doc Martins. Inside the circle, she carved a pentagram. Inside the pentagram, she lit a fire.

As the fire built she mixed her cauldron. It was a small black saucepan borrowed from her mum. Blood and hair were mixed with special berries and herbs, and the whole of it was crushed into a paste. It was a thick and lumpy paste, but it soon thinned and then ran smooth as she warmed it on the fire.

She read the magic words. She didn't know what they meant. She only recited. She used the phonetic guide that the book provided.

Only after did she realise that the words meant death. That she'd told the spirits to kill Tasha Barcroft. That

Tasha would die and she, Frigg, would take her place.

All she heard that night was the sound of her own voice and the fire crackling. When she'd finished the spell, she heard Merlin meow. She'd gone home and thrown the mixture in the river as she went.

She would like to say that that was the last time she played with magic. She'd like to pretend it ended there. But much worse would follow. Darker curses. Evil she couldn't even bear to remember.

The river was off limits now. Blue and white lines of police tape ran along the riverside. They fluttered like rubbish in the trees.

A policewoman stood on the bridge. She wore the black armour of the modern force, with a yellow high-vis stretched over it. She was worried about visibility, out there in the nothing.

Frigg approached, head bent.

'Good afternoon,' the policewoman nodded. 'Are you going over the bridge?'

Frigg nodded.

'Well I'm afraid there's been an incident,' the policewoman said, bluntly. 'Someone's fallen into the river and become stuck. Officers are working flat out to find a method of extraction but, for now, we have to warn the public not to try and get involved.'

She smiled at Frigg with a crooked, sympathetic smile.

'We don't want anyone else in there. One is trouble enough.'

Frigg nodded and stepped on to the bridge.

Her heart was beating fast. If the officer wasn't there she'd have looked down straight away, but now she was caught. She wanted to look with all her heart, but she was scared. Could she stop? How? How could she stop?

She walked over the bridge without looking and started to walk away along the path.

No. She told herself. Don't be silly.

The policewoman watched as Frigg stopped and turned around. The Goth girl walked back up to the bridge. As she stood there, at the foot of the bridge again, the officer noticed her hands were trembling in her hoody. Frigg stared at her shoes and bit her lip.

'Do you want to see the body?' the officer asked.

Frigg jumped. Put that way, it sounded so monstrous. *But yes,* she thought. *Yes, that is what I want. I want to see the body of the girl I killed.*

Frigg nodded.

The officer stood back and indicated with her arm that Frigg could approach. 'It's a free country,' the officer said. 'As much as we might prefer people not to look, there's no law against it.'

Frigg nodded. She mounted the bridge, grasped the crumbling stone with both hands. She leaned out over the water.

Tasha Barcroft was spread out beneath the ice.

She was there, caught, as if in mid-plunge. Her red hair splayed out behind her in autumnal folds. The loose fabric of her clothing had been frozen as it rippled in the water, rolling out around her like an aura. Her eyes, her lips, her face were almost blissful.

'She's beautiful,' Frigg whispered.

The girl she'd killed had been beautiful. Frigg saw this now. The girl who held her head under the tap as the water got hotter and hotter, scalding her face and scalp and neck. She had been beautiful. She was beautiful. The girl beneath the ice.

Frigg knew now why the police officer was there. There was something in Tasha's body, now that it was dead, that called out to her. She seemed to offer herself. Yes, even to Frigg; to Frigg, who had killed her. She offered herself and Frigg was filled with a desire to crawl out on to the ice and join her. She knew now perhaps what Lucas had felt. Or perhaps this too was different?

'She's beautiful,' Frigg whispered again.

She stared at her, and kept staring. The officer had laughed at first, but was now getting worried.

Ten minutes turned to fifteen and then to twenty. The officer stepped back, off the bridge, and left Frigg there with the body, alone. Whatever had been their relationship, she thought, it must have been a serious one. Actions are hard to predict around death, at least for an inexperienced cop.

The officer stood guard as Frigg gazed down from the bridge. She gazed down into the river, into Tasha's eyes, into Tasha Barcroft. The sun sank in the sky and the air grew heavy with more snow.

Chapter Eleven

——

Frigg McBride

Down by the river the sun set an hour before it truly left and the shadows crawled along the frozen valley long before the sky grew red.

Frigg stood in the darkness, leaning over the bridge, her dark hair and hoodie silhouetted like a tree stump against the snow.

She didn't move as the misted air took on the orange of sunset. Neither did she move when the last crimson light caught in the scattered ice; the forest lit like the dying embers of a bonfire.

She just stared down at Tasha Barcroft's body.

The police officer had been unnerved by Frigg. At first the Goth girl had just seemed curious. Then her curiosity turned morbid, grim, the policewoman must've thought. But then, the longer she stood watching, the more her actions seemed justifiable. She'd experienced a shock and this was her way of processing it.

The sun set. The frozen, blissful face of Tasha hadn't moved. Neither had Frigg's, who stood watching her.

The officer clicked on a torch.

'Alright,' she announced. 'I've got to get off. I'm meeting the relief constable up at the narrow passage. Up there.'

She pointed. Frigg turned vaguely back to look at her.

'If you see anything,' she continued. 'Just call out and we'll both be down here straightaway.

'If nothing happens, then the relief constable will be down in ten minutes. We just need to fill in some forms to sign off on the shift change. There's a new rota system, you see…'

Frigg turned back to the river. The officer waved her torch out over the forest, locating the path that led up and away. The Goth girl was harmless, she'd decided. There'd be no trouble.

In the dark, Tasha's face had all but disappeared.

The surface of the ice carried a light dusting of snow, but not enough to cloud the reflections of the sky above. Tasha's face was now only a collection of outlines to Frigg. She was a memory, wrapped in black cloud, with a scattering of powder on top.

There were girls who would be glad to know Tasha was dead. She'd been cruel, picking on the weak and the friendless.

She'd been insecure, perhaps, but what girl wasn't?

But those girls had probably forgotten all about Tasha Barcroft now. They had laughed at her death and would use it later to get sympathy.

Those girls, Frigg wondered, would they be able to face Tasha's body? Could they look down at those blissful, peaceful eyes and think those thoughts?

Those thoughts all seemed so small now, Frigg realised. All of the school drama. All of her feelings. Both their abundance and their absence. All of it was small compared to the girl beneath the ice.

'Did Lucas kill you?' Frigg asked.

It felt unlikely. He didn't seem capable. She thought of his petty frustrations; of his floppy fringe, and couldn't imagine him in a murderous fury.

But then there was a lot she couldn't imagine. She couldn't imagine his soft touch, or what it must have felt like for Tasha to have been with him.

She couldn't imagine death.

She used to close her eyes and think about not existing. Something always leaked in. Even if it was only her feet touching the ground, there was always something.

It was then that she heard it. Something. A rustle of leaves. The short, panicked snap of a twig beneath a heel.

'Hello?'

Frigg called out, apprehensive.

She was aware, all of a sudden, of the dark moving in close to her. It had formed up in walls like the snowdrifts which had grown in mere hours during the worst of the weather. The darkness had settled all around her, building black barriers of night.

'Is someone there?' she called again.

Silence. No appearance of anything moving. In many places, no appearances at all.

Adrenaline pumped through Frigg's system. Her eyes and ears started fooling her. She heard voices over there, whispers of wind caught in the trees, and then snapping – was it? – over there. She tried not to move, but still her eyes darted left and right.

She couldn't remember whether she'd really heard the sound. Only convinced herself she hadn't. Then, she heard it again.

A rustle. A click of boot on stone. The snap of a twig.

'Who's there?' Frigg called. She could hear the panic in her own voice as she spoke.

A horrible chill ran down her spine. She remembered the rituals – as if she could ever forget them; remembered the circles she'd drawn, and the pentagrams within. With horror, she realised that demons might be loose in the woods.

She called out again.

Hadn't the policewoman said she'd be back to help her? Hadn't she said she was listening?

'Hello?' her voice was high now. 'Hello!?'

Whatever demon it was, it approached her.

From the bushes, a dark figure came.

It was dressed in loose clothing, dark as Frigg's. She saw the outline of a hood and wild hair. She sniffed the air but could smell neither smoke nor sulphur. It stood twenty feet away. It looked male.

'Who are you?' she asked.

The figure scratched at its head. The light caught its sleeve. It was a hoody. It wore a hoody. The sound of scratching was that of human fingernails in human hair.

'Were you watching me?' she asked, her voice growing calmer.

Now she knew he wasn't a demon, she could hardly be scared of the man.

'I'm…' the man said, before trailing off.

He stood there, ragged. His voice low and   mumbling. He spoke like he was talking with a too-big tongue, or through a mouthful of marshmallows.

Frigg blinked. She raised a hand to peer at him.

'Who are you?' she repeated.

He coughed. It was a damp cough. A cough wet with cigarette smoke and walking in the rain.

'I'm Todd,' he said. 'Todd Morrow.'

Frigg nodded.

'I'm, like, the groundskeeper.' He coughed. 'Like, forest maintenance.'

'You look after the woods?' Frigg asked.

'Yeah,' he snorted and spat. Clearing his nostrils. 'Yeah, that's it.'

They stood silent for a moment. Frigg looked down at Tasha, or where she knew Tasha to be. It was too dark now to see anything. Then she looked up in the direction the police woman. Nobody was coming back down.

'I'm sorry for watching you,' the man mumbled. 'I was scared.'

'Scared?'

'They arrested me before,' Todd nodded. 'They said I'd killed her. They said they knew I did it, and they were going to send me to prison or the electric chair or something.'

'We don't have the electric chair in this country.'

Todd looked baffled. He scratched at his face. From the

sound, Frigg could tell he had a beard. Then, as he began stumbling towards her, a single shaft of moonlight passed for a moment through the clouds. The valley was illuminated.

She saw he was young. Under thirty, maybe twenty-five. He looked confused, but not dangerous.

'Why did they think you'd killed her?' Frigg asked.

'I don't know.'

Then, thinking about it, his face creased up. His whole body shook.

To his shoes he said. 'I guess because I like staring.'

Frigg looked at the young man and then down into the dark. She grew more confident as she saw his awkwardness. She felt sorry for him, almost. Sorry that a boy could end up how Todd had.

'I like staring too,' she said. 'It's not a crime.'

Todd nodded his head in agreement. Then, as she chanced a peek into the boy's eyes, she saw how green they were. Green like jewels in the night. In a landscape of black and white, darkening more with each moment, his eyes were bright.

'What's your name?' he asked.

'Frigg,' she muttered. 'People call me that.'

'Why do they call you that?'

'I don't know,' she shrugged. 'It's short for my full name I guess.'

'And what's that?' he asked.

'Frigite. Frigite McBride.'

The scruffy boy's eyes grew wide with dazed wonder.

'Those are beautiful names. You shouldn't be ashamed of them.'

Then, as he scratched his tangled hair again, he asked. 'Would it be okay if I called you Frigite?'

Frigg swallowed.

'No,' she said, her mouth working automatically.

'I mean… maybe? I guess so.'

'Frigite,' Todd began, and took a step towards her.

She jumped, startled.

Knowing her reaction had hurt him, she took a step forward. This seemed to calm him. For someone so loose and uncoordinated in his movements, Frigg thought, Todd was certainly skittish.

'If you want, Frigite, we could have some soup?'

'What?'

Todd's eyes showed confusion. It had been a long time since he'd had to explain his thoughts.

'I live up the valley. There's an old building there, like a stone thing. I live in there. I make soup out of the tubers that get stuck under the ice. I dry the herbs in the autumn. I have those too. If you want to, you can come and have some soup.'

Then, as if shocked that he'd asked, he went silent. He stared at the floor again. He stared down at his own boots, sodden as they were with meltwater, and scuffed by rocks and brambles

'I have to feed my cat,' Frigg said, again automatically.

'But,' she thought aloud. 'Perhaps I could have some soup first. Just one bowl. Then I'll go.'

Todd nodded and, a moment later, beamed. His wonky smile was contagious. Frigg found herself warmed.

Although it was perhaps not so much his smile, but the thrill of him. A man of the woods. An outcast.

Todd turned and walked.

'Where are you going?' Frigg asked, following along behind.

'Up the valley,' he said. 'I live up the valley.'

'Okay. I'll follow.'

The two figures made their slow and trudging way up the valley. Frigg was mesmerised by the route that Todd took. One moment he'd be following a path, the next he'd crash straight through a snowbank. Sometimes old and forgotten pathways converged with his own in-built sense of direction and at other times he seemed to be moving without any sense of his surroundings at all, wading through bushes and vaulting over low walls, following some rigid internal compass. Frigg couldn't tell if it was the newly-frozen snow covering Todd's tracks, or whether he was merely following his instincts.

Frigg had, until that evening, thought of herself as a natural forest-dweller. Only now had she realised what it truly meant. Todd was like one of the ancients. He walked as if he'd never seen a road, as if fences meant nothing.

It was only after they skimmed along the top of some stones, crossing a natural ford in the river, that Frigg spoke again.

'So, what do you do, Todd? Do you just live out here?'

'I told you!' Todd furrowed his brows. 'I'm like a kind of forest ranger or something.'

'You don't sound very certain.'

There was an impatient edge to his voice that she didn't like.

'Well it was a long time ago when I got the job.'

He kicked a pile of brambles.

'I don't remember the details of it.'

Frigg stepped over the brambles. Her Doc Martins scraped through the thorns.

'Do they pay you?' she asked.

'I guess,' Todd said.

Stopping, he turned and caught Frigg by the arm.

'Frigite, look! That's my house!'

She was shocked at the sudden physical contact and then, barely recovered, gasped at the structure Todd pointed out.

It was small, tiny even. So small she would never have thought a living person could survive there. It looked like it was built to store firewood, or to hide from the rain. It didn't look habitable.

But it did look inhabited. The dry-stone walls were overgrown with ivy, but it was meticulously tended. As they approached she saw he'd plaited the ivy's strands around the doorway, forming a living frame.

'It's like a fairy's house,' she laughed.

Todd frowned. 'What do you mean?'

'Oh,' she touched his arm. 'Nothing. It's really nice.'

Now it was his turn to shrink from a touch.

'Okay,' he said. 'Well, if you come in then I'll make us the soup. Then you can go.'

'Okay.'

Inside the tiny dwelling it was even more like a fairy

tale, Frigg thought. Dried herbs and plants of all sorts hung from the narrow rafters and a crooked pile of firewood sat in one corner with clothes drying on it.

There was room enough for one person to sit and make a fire. Neither could stand at full height. The air inside had an intense smell: woodsmoke, body odour, and sweet herbs.

'Where do you sleep?' Frigg asked.

Todd ignored her. He was scratching at the ground, collecting up scraps of hay and old newspapers. She heard the flick of a lighter and, within seconds, the whole room was illuminated. The crackle of flames and the flicker of orange light reminded Frigg of her spell.

The lump twisted in her belly. She tried to shrug it off or swallow it down but she didn't know how. Instead, she shuffled into the one chair that Todd owned; a foldable plastic one meant for camping.

Did he sleep in this, Frigg wondered?

'It'll be warm enough in a minute,' Todd said.

He was squatting by the fireside, rubbing his hands together, pointing them at the flame. Occasionally he blew.

'Do you not have anywhere to sit?' she asked him.

'No,' he shook his head. 'Don't have visitors. Just need one chair.'

Frigg watched the firelight playing over the boy's wild and scruffy face. His eyes, even in this light, glowed pure green.

'I've only got one chair. One pot. One mug.' He repeated. 'You can have soup first. Then you can go. I'll have soup after.'

Frigg pulled her hoody down over her knees. The heat reminded her of the cold. The light reminded her of the darkness. It was dark and cold and her mum was probably wondering where she was. She would leave soon and would say she went back to Erin's.

'That's a problem with being on your own,' he said.

He shook his head. She could see in his eyes that he was starting to grow resentful. She knew the feeling. Too much thought. On your own, you got swamped in it, saturated. Frozen under it.

'When you're on your own,' he finished her thought for her. 'You've got to do everything yourself. Nobody helps you. Nobody likes you. People don't like people who are on their own. They only like   people who are like them.'

Todd caught her eye.

'I didn't kill her,' he said.

His eyes narrowed then. He looked threatening.

'I know,' she nodded. 'I didn't either.'

He looked at her strangely. Had she offended him? Perhaps she had.

He took down a mug from a hook and poured some lumpy liquid into it. It was the soup, she realised. In the dark it looked jet black.

He went to the door and brought in a huge clump of snow. He set the mug over the fire and dropped chunk after chunk of hard snow into it. The snow melted, forming water; water thickening to broth.

'I'm alone too,' Frigg whispered as Todd worked. 'You

don't have to be worried.'

Todd's face turned sad. He prodded the melting snow with mournful eyes.

'I'm not worried,' he said eventually. 'I have nothing to worry about.'

Frigg nodded. He was right. Nothing to worry about. She had nothing, too. No feelings, it seemed. Nothing to keep her on this earth. And yet she worried. She was stricken with guilt. She had, she knew, killed Tasha; or at least brought her death into being. But there was no one who could prove it. No-one who would even believe her. It was nothing. Her act of murder had been nothing. This, among all her nothings, all the nothingness in the world was what she feared most. Her greatest and all-consuming worry was nothing.

'I think I know what you mean,' Frigg smiled in the firelight. 'I think I feel that too.'

When he finally passed her the soup, she made sure to touch his hand when she took it. A shiver ran down his skin. The soup was delicious. It tasted of warmth, and of safety.

Chapter Twelve

Inspector Todor

Todor stood in the corner of the interrogation room.

His arms were folded in front of his chest and with one upraised hand he rubbed nervously at his chin and cheek.

An outside observer would be forgiven for thinking the Inspector was the one being interrogated. Indeed, he pushed himself into that corner like a cornered cat, not speaking but waiting, in silence, eyes darting.

Across from him was Lucas Farringdon. The boy was pale, his gaze fixed on the table top. He stared out of sunken, exhausted eyes at nothing in particular.

'So,' Todor repeated for what must've been the fifteenth time. 'You say you couldn't have killed Miss Barcroft because you were at home with your father.'

Lucas nodded.

'How many times do I have to say it, Lucas?' Todor was almost begging. 'You have to speak. The tape can't hear you if you nod.'

'Yes,' Lucas sighed.

'Yes what?'

'Yes, I was a home with my dad. There was a blizzard.

We live high up on the hill. We'd been trapped inside for two weeks.'

Todor rubbed his chin again.

'But the only person who can back you up on this is your father himself?'

'And my mum,' Lucas whispered.

'I've told you, Lucas,' Todor was pleading again. 'If your mother was upstairs and in a state of... reduced capacity, then she can't serve as a reliable witness. Why, you could have been out the entire time, provided you popped upstairs once a day to say hello. In fact, by the sounds of it, you didn't even do that.'

'No,' Lucas shook his head. 'Why would I?'

'Oh, I don't know, Lucas.'

Todor unfolded his arms and passed a hand through his hair.

Lucas Farringdon retreated again into his silence.

The interrogation room at the Avon Murray police station was a minimal affair, reserved mostly for paperwork and the occasional Christmas party fling. As Todor was told on his first day; the police knew who the criminals were and the criminals knew what was required of them. There were no interrogations. Nothing beyond a cursory half-hour for the sake of appearances.

Now, as Lucas sat in the hard-plastic chair for his eighth hour, Todor regretted the laxness of the station he inherited. It looked like a school cafeteria. It had an identical table, in fact, to those Lucas would've eaten his sandwiches at.

The light was too sterile. The chairs made a silly squeaking noise when you shifted your weight. The interrogation felt closer to school detention than a murder inquiry.

'And your father was the one that found the body?'

'Apparently,' Lucas shrugged.

Todor rubbed his eyes.

'A positive or negative response will be sufficient, Lucas. Yes or no.'

'*You* said that *he* found the body,' Lucas said, annoyance creeping into his quiet voice. '*He* didn't tell *me* anything like that. Just that Tasha was dead. So, I don't know, do I?'

He blinked a number of times, lifting a hand to shield his eyes from the light.

'That's what I think, anyway. I don't know. I can't remember properly.'

'You can't remember properly,' Todor nodded.

The Inspector rubbed at his temples. They were both tired. Exhausted, even. And it was leading them nowhere.

Why was he there again, speaking to this boy?

Well, he was the girl's boyfriend. That much everyone could admit. They'd had fights, he'd said, but nothing that was serious. They hadn't been fighting when she was murdered.

So, what?

Well, the grandmother, who was the girl's guardian and a pillar of the community, was certain it was the boy. She was certain, too, that it wasn't the homeless lad who lived in the woods, as much as he seemed the natural candidate.

So, what?

The Inspector supposed that the boy's testimony was flawed. The only witness to his alibi was his   father, and the father, William, was unreliable. After all, he was the man who found the body.

Yet, it *really was* snowing heavily these past weeks. The weather warnings were still in place. Being snowed in was more than credible.

So, what?

What am I saying? The Inspector asked himself. That the boy snuck out in a snowstorm to kill his girlfriend and then his father helped him to cover it up… by reporting it?

Or that the grandmother, pillar of the community, Mrs Barcroft, was wrong, or lying?

Or, third option, most likely but worst of all: that the murderer was still on the loose and the Inspector had absolutely no idea who it could be?

'We'll have to wait for the autopsy,' Todor nodded to himself. 'When they finally get the body out then we'll have our answers.'

Lucas nodded. He didn't meet Todor's gaze. He stared on at the small pile of nothing on the table. He'd stared at the same pile for hours now.

'Yes,' he confirmed.

'Yes, what?' Todor asked.

'Yes,' Lucas nodded. 'When you get the body, then you'll see. You'll find out who did it and that it wasn't me. I didn't do it.'

He leaned forward, crossing his arms and sinking his head into them.

'I didn't do anything. Not a thing. *Nothing.*'

Inspector Todor walked to the door. He unlocked it, opened it, and held it open.

'Everyone's done something, Lucas,' he sighed. 'Now let's get out of here.'

Lucas didn't wait to be asked again. He thrust the squeaky plastic chair back and strode out of the door, his head held high now in defiance. Inspector Todor, by contrast, was stooped, broken looking. The older man had a five o'clock shadow while the young boy seemed totally refreshed.

As they walked down the corridor they passed the duty sergeant. Her eyes passed up and down the young suspect and then repeated the action on the Inspector.

Todor could feel himself being weighed up. He could sense the judgement of the inferior ranks. Only weeks ago, he'd been among them. Now, in his great incompetence, he'd been elevated. It was only natural that they suspected him. A ghost hung over him   always. The shadow of his own inadequacy.

Todor looked more and more haunted as the hours went by.

A murder. No clear suspect. And the body was still under the ice.

They'd tried. God how they'd tried to find a way. The snow had made everything impossible. After the two officers ended up in hospital – they were still there, recovering from frostbite-induced shock – putting people on the ice was ruled out. The valley was too steep for heavy equipment.

The foliage was too dense for a helicopter. Everything else was ruled out by the never-ending snow and ice.

We're stuck, Todor told himself. *Or should I say, I'm stuck? Inspector Dafydd Todor. A man in charge of an investigation and without a single clue.*

William Farringdon was waiting in the reception area with Scout. As the Inspector walked Lucas down the hall, following along on the boy's coattails, he noticed the man and his dog up ahead. He felt his cheeks reddening.

'Lucas!' William called out. 'Bloody good to see you! You told them how it was, eh?'

Scout leapt up and barked. Her tail wagged furiously.

'Scout's missed you, lad!' William beamed.

Lucas smiled at his dad.

'They're letting me go!' Lucas grinned.

He ran into his father's outstretched arms and the two of them held each other tight; slapping each other's backs in a display of manly affection. Todor shrank to see it.

'Lucas is right,' the Inspector said. 'We're letting him go. For now. His alibi is not concrete by any means, but it's enough to alleviate suspicion for the moment.'

William patted his son one more time on the back and then, as he looked over the boy's shoulder at the Inspector, his face fell.

'I'd sincerely like to know what you're playing at,' William snapped. 'Bringing him in on suspicion of murder? For God's sake, man, don't you just bring people in for questioning anymore?'

'I was…' Todor flubbed. 'It *was* questioning, I…'

'Have we ever done anything to indicate that we wouldn't comply with the police's requests?' William added.

His finger itched. It was very close to pointing. Once the pointing started, it would soon turn to jabbing.

'The Farringdons have had a spotless history. Long before we came to this town we've been pillars of society. Law abiding citizens. And to receive this treatment, like common criminals?'

Inspector Todor's hands moved inexorably towards his trouser pockets. They scrambled into them like two white mice running from a cat.

'Do you know what you've done, eh?' William asked.

Todor was silent.

'It's okay dad,' Lucas touched his father's arm, as if holding him back.

'It's not okay!'

William's finger lifted. As he spoke he pointed it to himself, then his son, and then the world outside. Todor knew that he would be on its receiving end next.

'The whole town has been talking,' William shouted. 'My wife's received phone calls. She's not a well woman, Inspector, as you well know! As I walked Scout down to the shops I heard them talking. I heard the whispers, saw the meaningful looks. They think we're murderers!'

'I'm very-'

'Murderers, Inspector!' William snapped. 'And all of it because you just *had* to make a big scene of bringing Lucas in. I hear you're new here, is that right? Trying to prove yourself a regular Sherlock Holmes, are you?

Solve the case right off the bat, is that it? Well you've muddied our name, Inspector, and I've no doubt you've muddied your own now as well. If you were going by instinct then your instincts are lousy, and the police here must know it!'

The finger had come up. It was jabbing the air every other syllable, pointing straight for Todor's chest.

Inspector Todor turned around. He saw the receptionist, pretending not to watch. What was that in her eyes? Was she laughing at him? Was he humiliated? He turned back to the Farringdons and saw the old man fuming and the young one holding him back.

Some Inspector you are, Todor. The boy is the one protecting you, after all you've laid on him these past hours.

Suddenly, Todor felt winded. Entirely exhausted and light-headed like he was about to pass out.

Scout padded cautiously up to the Inspector. Surprised, the Inspector looked down at it. He raised an eyebrow. The dog looked up, turning her head on one side.

'I shall expect a full apology for this,' William was saying. 'If not immediately, then as soon as the investigation has been resolved. I want it known that my boy is entirely without blame.'

The Inspector crouched down and lifted up his hand. Scout moved close to him and rubbed her nose against the outstretched palm. With his other hand, Todor rubbed her hairy neck.

'You aren't from here, Inspector, so you might not understand,' William continued. 'But out here in the country they're a suspicious lot. It took years for them to finally accept us as residents. Knowing we'd come from the city was enough to have us blackballed from every social gathering, outcast from every social group. We had finally ingratiated our way in – or so we thought. Now we'll be back out again, I'm sure.'

'Dad, it's okay,' Lucas tugged his father's sleeve. 'It's okay. Let's just go home.'

'It's not okay,' William turned to his son now. 'I can hear them already. I can hear them in my head. I can see their nasty, twisted up little faces! "*No smoke without fire*," they'll be saying. "*No smoke without fire*"; like it's a bloody mantra. Like the fact that it's a recognised turn of phrase must mean that on *all* occasions it must be true!'

'You're getting carried away, dad.'

He tried to pacify his father with a smile. The older man's eyes, he noticed, were bloodshot. There was a sagginess to his eyelids.

'I'm not getting carried away,' William said, though his voice stuttered a little. 'You were the one they arrested. It's your name they blackened. You're the one they kept in a cell for hours…'

'Yes,' Lucas nodded. 'And now I'm the one who would rather you drop it and let us go home.'

'Good girl,' Inspector Todor said.

The Inspector had advanced from rubbing Scout's hairy neck to hugging her and then scratching her upturned belly. Dogs had a natural affection for the

Welshman. He'd never had one of his own. The job was too rigorous. He felt cruel thinking of an animal locked up at home all day. Animals should be wild and free.

The Inspector rubbed at Scouts belly while she made a series of gurgling, yapping sounds. She rolled left and right and her tail wagged against the plastic floor tiles.

'She's a good girl,' Todor said in a doggy voice. 'A very good girl.'

William, caught between the puppy dog eyes of his son and the doggy talk of the Inspector, sighed and accepted his fate.

'Well, I suppose the truth will out in time,' he nodded. 'Our innocence shall be vindicated. The people will take us back. Eventually. I suppose.'

Lucas nodded. 'They will, dad. And if not, who cares? I can go off to uni like Jo. We can stick to our bit of the hill. We have everything we need. Oh, I don't know…'

Lucas held his head. The weight of everything kept crashing in on him.

After his endless interrogation he felt submerged. Todor has seen the look before like the boy was in a submarine, having to keep out all of the tragedy and the horror. All the grim reality, the fact that Tasha's body was still there, trapped in the ice. It was like water, an ocean of feeling they were sinking into it. Deeper and deeper. You could plug every leak, but every now and then the hull ruptured. The horror of it rushed in. Soon Lucas Farringdon would have to hit the bottom and soon he would have to brave the deep.

'I really need to go, dad' Lucas said again. 'I want to go home.'

'Alright.'

William had put his pointing finger away now.

Todor rubbed his fingers one more time behind Scout's ear and stood up.

'I'll do the best I can,' he said. 'We'll find the killer. If it's not your boy, then he's got nothing to worry about. I personally don't think it's him. Not anymore. Who it could be though… well, that's anybody's guess at the moment.'

William attached Scout's lead and turned to go.

'That doesn't fill me with hope, Inspector,' he said. 'That gives me no hope at all, in fact.'

As the blue door swung shut behind them, Todor turned back to the secretary. Her face was unreadable, as always. *What did she think of him?* He wondered.

He wondered what they all thought. He didn't think much of himself.

If it wasn't for the promise of an autopsy – the small hope that some way, somehow, they could extract the frozen body – then the trail would have gone, very literally, dead cold.

Inspector Todor straightened his tie and turned to go back to his office. Then, thinking better of it, he went to the coat rack and pulled on his greatcoat. He slid his wallet from the inside pocket and checked his credentials were all in place. He walked out.

'I'm going to the pathologists,' Todor called to the still-passive receptionist. 'Patch through any calls.'

Chapter Thirteen

Doctor Drąg

Avon Murray and its surrounding areas had no dedicated pathologist. Instead, the police used the services of the local undertaker.

Back in Poland, Zygmunt Drąg had served some time as a coroner. It was back in the communist era, when the difference between a qualified professional and an enthusiastic amateur was nowhere as important as the difference between those who were in and out of the Party.

Drąg was out of the Party. He'd always been out of it. Had he ever wanted to be in, there would have been no chance. He had too many black marks against his name.

He left Poland in 2005, part of that first big wave of twenty-first century migration; thousands of Central Europeans travelling across the EU looking for work, only to return six months later feeling largely disillusioned.

Drąg didn't go back, he'd stayed, and, in time, the people of Avon Murray came to trust him as their local undertaker. Sometime after that, the police contacted him, asking if he would act as a pathologist as well.

Occasionally the police found a body, usually of someone

old and abandoned. A cursory check was needed to confirm no foul play. Drąg could perform this task easily, and did so with enough thoroughness and professionalism to ensure his employer's confidence.

They never asked for his credentials. They knew he had none. As long as the task was done, and was seen to be done, then they were happy.

The funeral parlour was situated just off the main road, separated from the town by few fields and a clump of trees. It overlooked the same river that ran down from the valley. By the time it reached the undertaker's, its ice had melted. It ran by Drąg's window, reduced now to a crystal-clear trickle between frost-topped rocks.

The snow still fell there, but it fell evenly, and thin.

He heard Todor's boots crackle across the front lawn. The snow was less than two inches down there, he thought to himself.

Zygmunt Drąg opened his door and leaned against the frame.

'You look cold, officer! May I offer you something to warm you up? A cup of tea perhaps?'

The Inspector looked up bleary-eyed.

He was tall, almost too tall, with a weather-beaten look that made him, for all his sixty-something years, look statuesque, potent, virile even. A wild mane of grey sprouted from his head. He looked over the top of his small, round glasses as if demonstrating how little he needed them.

'Don't suppose you have coffee?' Todor asked, trying not

to shiver.

'I am afraid not,' Drąg smiled. 'I gave it up when I came to this country. The English didn't know what to do with it back then. It is getting better, but it is still not to my tastes.'

'A tea will do then,' Todor said. 'It's been a long day.'

'So, I hear,' Drąg nodded. 'Come on in.'

They walked through the pinewood office to the living space at the rar. Todor doubtlessly noted the wide variety of crosses that Drąg kept. They stood on shelves and hung pendulously from silver chains. In a cabinet in the corner there was a menorah and a pile of religious clothing of indeterminate faith.

'You know Jesus Christ once said to let the dead bury the dead.' Drąg laughed. 'I'm not dead, but   perhaps I look suitably grim eh? You see you cannot smile at a funeral, officer, even when it's your fourth one that day. It is my job to look mournful. If you look mournful often enough, the habit sticks.'

They passed through some bead curtains and into a room that smelled of smoke and old leather.

'They called Don Quixote the Knight of the Mournful Face, you know.'

The pathologist swept a pile of magazines into the bin. He rounded the kitchen cabinet to the kettle.

'It was a pun, I think. To the Quixote it reflected his mourning, his longing for his lady love, the sweet Dulcinea. For the rest of us, it meant that his face, to look upon it, was enough to make you sad.'

Drąg laughed.

'An ugly man!'

The Inspector glanced around at the leather chairs. An inspector would stand, he supposed. And so, the inspector stood.

Todor noticed a dog bowl.

'Ah, you have a dog?'

'Yes. She is called Rosie. She is a nizinny. I do not know the English name.'

'A nizinny?' Todor nodded. 'I was thinking of getting a dog maybe. I'd like one.'

Drąg clicked the kettle on and stared, long and mournful-eyed at the Inspector. Folk couldn't shake the feeling that it was death watching them. A dead soul watching and judging him for what they were choosing to do with life.

To spend your living hours chasing around the dead… Perhaps Christ had been on to something?

'I can bring her through if you like. She has been coming and going into the back field all day. Rosie keeps the crows away. I don't want them here. They accentuate what doesn't need accentuating.'

He rubbed his chin.

'By which I mean the death.'

'It's okay.'

Todor got the sense that if the pathologist's dog didn't like him, then he'd have a hard time with the pathologist too.

Drąg rubbed his hands together. The kettle clicked.

'No problem,' he said. 'We will keep Rosie in the

garden, hunting her avian prey. We will have tea and we will discuss the matter that brings you to my door.'

He lifted the kettle and poured.

'We have not met before, no?'

'No.'

Todor perched himself on the edge of a leather chair. He looked sheepish, ready to spring up should the pathologist say something.

'No, I don't think we've met. I'm new here.'

'You have a strange accent,' Drąg said.

'I'm from Gresynu, in Wales,' Todor nodded. 'You know, back in Wales everyone says I don't have an accent. I used to get bullied for talking posh, I did. It's funny how things come around.'

The pathologist passed the Inspector his tea.

It was steaming hot, still boiling. Todor set it down. Drąg, not noticing the heat, held it to his lips and reflected.

'There are accents in Polish, but I do not recall if any is considered posh.'

He sipped from the boiling water. Todor flinched watching.

'I think this must be an English condition. Your love of class perhaps? We do have a formal diction. But it's more about word choices than pronunciation.'

Todor nodded.

'You see, officer…'

'It's Inspector.'

'You see, Inspector,' he continued unfazed. 'If I were to

be polite to you, as you are my employer and, in many ways, my superior, I should say: "*Would Mr Inspector like the tea?*". That is not quite a correct translation, as we do not have the definite article, but you understand the sense of it?'

The Inspector nodded. He wrapped his fingers around the handle of his mug and felt them searing. He gave up on it for the moment.

'Do you speak Welsh, Inspector? I hear it is a beautiful language.'

'No. Look, Mister, erm, Drang...'

The pathologist nodded, receptive.

'Mister Drang, we have a body. We're going to need a post-mortem. It's not the usual kind that you deal with here. You see, there's been a murder.'

Drąg's face was mournful, but his eyes glinted. Professional curiousity, perhaps?

'Now, I'm going to warn you, Mister Drang, that there will be a lot riding on this post-mortem. So far, we have nothing but circumstantial evidence. We have suspects, but neither of them are obviously guilty. There may be a third out there, or a fourth, with equal likelihood of committing the crime. The crime scene turned up nothing. With the damn snow everything's frozen over. If there are any traces left of the crime, they will be left on the body itself.'

'I see...' Drąg nodded.

His nodding seemed to be a habit. It was his way of processing information. He would wander through his house, nodding.

The living area overlapped with the funeral parlour. It was as if the two parts of the building were both the same to him. His nodding, as he walked around the crosses and the coffins, carried, in itself, a touch of the religious.

The Inspector's tea had finally cooled enough to drink. The pathologist had already finished his. He set the empty mug beside the kettle.

After a moment of silence, Drąg spoke.

'So where is this body?'

'This is the problem…'

'It is the one in the river, yes?'

Todor's eyes narrowed.

'How did you know?'

Drąg gave the Inspector a pitying glance.

'Do you know how small Avon Murray is,   Inspector? Do you know how quickly news travels? Even someone like myself, the last one in town to be invited to anything, has already known for hours about the murder.

'In fact,' he rubbed his white-stubbled chin. 'When I was told by the postwoman about the case, she said it was a rich boy, one who lives up in a mansion by the High Woods, who did it.'

The Inspector's head sank down into his hands. William Farringdon was right. He shouldn't have brought the boy in as a suspect. No real inspector would have done such a thing. He sighed into his palms.

'It's not a mansion…' the Inspector managed to say. 'I've been to the house and it's not…'

Inspector Todor sighed and rubbed his face. He sipped from the tea again. He changed tack.

'You get post down here?'

'I have had it for three days.' Drąg sniffed. 'In summer it is a mere forty-minute walk from this house to the high woods. Now that distance is as great as between night and day, between the winter and the spring.'

Todor looked out of the window at the lightly falling snow.

'I'd not call this spring, but I get your point. Up in the hills it's impassable.'

'Impassable for the living,' Drąg raised an eyebrow. 'But for the dead?'

The Inspector shook his head.

'Whatever goes for the living goes twice for the dead.'

He scratched the back of his head and looked around at the religious trinkets. Even back there in the kitchen, they littered the walls. Death makes you face up to things. Being around it made you philosophical.

'We can't get her out,' he shrugged. 'We can't do it.'

'She is trapped in the ice?' Drąg nodded.

'Trapped.' Todor sniffed. 'Frozen solid. We can't get in there with equipment. We can't get close. We tried with officers but...'

Drąg was nodding. The news had no doubt reached him about that first accident too. But he had other things on his mind.

'So what state is the body in?'

Inspector Todor furrowed his brows.

'Well, she's frozen so...'

'Frozen?' Drąg nodded. 'And before then, murdered? Yes?'

Todor nodded. 'We presume so.'

'*Presume...*' Drąg leant back and crossed his arms. 'Now there is a strange word choice. It would seem to me that one would presume nothing until one had the evidence, but then I am no officer of the law.'

'The police have to work on our presumptions, Mister Drang. It's the courts who consider suspects innocent until proven guilty. We have to act on our hunches. If there's no evidence, we can't just write it off as an accident. We have to find the evidence.'

'And if it's not there?'

That playful glint in the undertaker's eye again.

'And if there's no evidence, then we keep going. Either evidence will come about, or we will proceed to the next case.'

Drąg almost smiled

'It does not sound like a very satisfying job. Working always with this irresolution. Your life seems full of uncertainties, Inspector. It provides little certainty.'

The Inspector finished his tea and stood up.

'It certainly lacks the certainties of your job, Mister Drang. It's one of the two big certainties in life, isn't it? This and taxes?'

'To the contrary, Inspector,' Drąg's lips cracked at the corners. 'There is nothing certain about death. Outside of its happening, of course. But when it happens, how, why... death is the last great mystery, Inspector. In many ways, it is the only mystery. If it weren't for death, why,

I don't think any of us could bear to keep living at all. Without death, there would be no questions left to answer. None that matter.'

'Will you come to see the body?'

'No.'

The Inspector sighed.

'Why not?'

'I am an old man.'

Drąg closed his eyes.

'I am too old to be wandering around in a snowstorm.'

The Inspector made as if to walk out, before turning.

'So, what are we going to do then?'

Drąg spoke, his eyes still closed.

'I have a good imagination, Inspector. It comes from having seen many things in life. Why don't you describe her to me? This poor girl, who you say has been murdered. Tell me what she looks like?'

The Inspector looked down at his watch. The day was drawing to a close. There was little chance of anything happening once the town went to bed. In small towns, you ran on small town time. If he were to get anything out of today it would only be through this strange man.

'Okay,' he began. 'So, she was called Tasha. Tasha Barcroft. She had long red hair. Pale complexion. Her grandmother is a respected member of the community. She has the same eyes.'

'With respect,' Drąg's face was again mournful. 'As beneficial as such details may be, I am interested more in the pathological elements. Stab wounds. Bruising.

Broken bones. Things of that nature.'

'Okay, okay,' the Inspector swallowed. 'Well, if I'm going to be a hundred percent honest with you, Mister Drang...'

He found it hard to find the words. He didn't want it to sound the way that it inevitably would sound.

'To be honest with you, I looked down from the bridge. I saw she was frozen. I saw her long hair splayed out around her in red. I saw a peaceful, almost blissful look in her eyes. I saw her skin was white-'

'White?'

'White,' the Inspector nodded. 'And unbroken, unbruised. Entirely undamaged.'

Drąg's eyebrows knitted. He'd stopped nodding and was silent, face furrowed, as if listening to far off music.

The Inspector continued. 'I saw a young girl who was entirely in one piece. Not a bruise on her. Unless, of course, her dress was hiding them.'

'No puncture wounds? No stabbing or slashing? No gunshot wounds?' Drąg asked. 'No broken bones? No lacerations? No black eyes or broken teeth? Not even a look of terror or pain? No pupil dilation?'

'I can't say about the pupils,' the Inspector shrugged. 'I can't recall that level of detail. It was dark. I couldn't see everything.'

Drąg had opened his eyes and was staring now, furiously, at the Inspector.

The Inspector concluded his statement. 'But, yes, if asked, I would say that she was unharmed. Entirely undamaged. Not a scratch on her. Her appearance was blissful; the look of someone at total peace with the world.'

Zygmunt Drąg stared at Inspector Todor. Silence. Somewhere, in the snow-topped grass of the rear field, Rosie began to bark. Perhaps scaring away one of the hated crows. The pathologist stared at the Inspector and wouldn't break his gaze.

In response, Todor felt his hands return to his pockets. He felt himself shrug. He didn't like being looked at like this.

'If you're wondering why it's a murder, then don't ask me. I just took the case up. It was the reporting officer who said murder. Now I think about it, I don't know… I guess… Well, I just don't know…'

'That's right,' Drąg nodded. 'You don't know. None of us do. But you, well, you don't even know the significance of your own statements!'

'What do you mean?'

Drąg took off his glasses and rubbed the bridge of his nose.

'How to explain? Hmm. Well, Inspector, have you ever eaten a meal so delicious that you wanted to save it for later, and so you put it in the freezer?'

'I guess.'

'And have you ever picked blackberries and thought. 'Well, they have these in the freezers in the shops so maybe I can freeze them too."

'I can't say if I have or haven't,' the Inspector thought. 'But maybe I have.'

'What happens to food you freeze, Inspector?'

Drąg gave Todor a meaningful look.

'It comes out,' Todor struggled for the word. 'Sloppy, I guess.'

'Correct.' Drąg nodded. 'You see, freezing has the effect of shrinking nearly every physical material, whether organic or inorganic, except for one. A most important one for life on this Earth, Inspector-'

'Water,' the Inspector nodded now. 'Water expands when frozen.'

'That it does.' Drąg confirmed. 'And when all of your tissues contract, and the water in your body expands; then you end up like those sloppy dinners, Inspector. You burst like a blackberry.'

The Inspector held his breath for a moment, thinking about it, and perhaps not understanding. A visible chill went down his spine, and not winter chill.

'So, if blackberries burst when you put them in your freezer, then how do they freeze the frozen ones?' the Inspector asked. 'You know; the ones at the shop?'

'Liquid nitrogen.'

Drąg waved away the Inspector's baffled look.

'But it would not have the same effect on a human body. You are not to look for a madman carrying around liquid nitrogen, Inspector. The blackberries were merely an analogy. I felt they were sufficiently visceral for the kind of mess that you would expect to find if you were to encounter a *normal* body frozen in the ice.'

The Inspector swallowed. 'A *normal* one? You think

Tasha Barcroft isn't normal?'

'I did not know the girl,' Drag blinked. 'But by the sounds of things, her body, in its current state, is most unnatural. You have two options, Inspector.'

Inspector Todor nodded, listening.

'One: that a most unusual set of circumstances has led to this body being preserved in its current, seemingly unblemished state. Something worthy of a scientific paper, perhaps.'

'And two?'

The Inspector's hand shivered in its pocket.

'Two?'

Drag turned, picked up the Inspector's mug and carried it over to the sink. He let the water run for a few seconds. He dabbed his fingers under the stream, feeling it warm up.

'Why, option two, is the supernatural.'

'The supernatural?'

The pathologist was busy washing up his mugs.

'Indeed,' he nodded again. 'For the preservation of any frozen human body in the state that you describe cannot be accounted for by nature. Not unless it is some aspect of nature never before observed by man. So, it is either a very rare natural phenomenon, or one whose causes lie beyond the natural world. The realm beyond the natural, Inspector, is the supernatural. This is my observation.'

The Inspector pulled on his overcoat. In his panic he was barely aware of putting it on, and so, patting his pockets, he proceeded to look around the room for it for the next few seconds. Realising he was already wearing the coat, he turned to the pathologist, who was now drying his mugs and mumbling, seemingly at a cross above the sink. He bid him farewell.

'When you do get the body out,' Drąg said as he left. 'Try to get it here in one piece. I would be eager to inspect it.'

Chapter Fourteen

Mrs Barcroft

Mrs Barcroft looked in the mirror. She felt shrunken; a body which had kept her upright for all of these years, hidden under layers of dark fabric, and finally revealing itself through feelings. In the moment of her grief, she'd become human.

She looked at her frailty in the mirror, watched the deep crevices of her skin as her mouth moved. She saw the way her bones protruded. Was this all that was left of her?

She'd been awake all night and taken herself to bed at six o'clock after the exhaustion of the previous day. Yet, in retreating from the sunlight so soon, she'd set herself up for a terrible night.

She awoke at a quarter to eight, the daylight she'd sought to leave still there on the horizon, lingering on the day of her granddaughter's death.

She tried again, but it was no good. She wanted that sweet moment of forgetfulness; when you wake up, forgetting what sent you to bed.

Now she was no longer sleeping, and felt that even in her dreams she wouldn't sleep again. The knowledge of her loss, forever present and unsleeping.

The hours ground on and rest came strangely and in fits.

She found her house transformed. The alchemy of death turning every item – hairbrushes, discarded hairclips, loose socks – into talismans. Her granddaughter's things.

They'd gone the way of her daughter's belongings. No, not the same way, but similar. Both were lost, only now Tasha was lost for good.

The old bungalow was stark and unwelcoming in its furnishings. She desired neatness above all else. White walls and maroon carpets, plain wooden side tables and sofas that, for all their many pillows, gave little comfort.

Perhaps it'd been no place for children. Neatness and order, above all else, brought virtue. Sin was messy and neatness was clean.

The sun wasn't yet through the curtains when she leaned forward, toward the mirror, and scratched mascara onto her eyes.

She usually admired the first beams of cream-coloured light as they dropped across her kitchen table, but she wouldn't eat breakfast today.

She'd have a small black coffee and watch the day open.

Soon she'd have to remove the talismans. Perhaps after work?

Work. She must go to work. The parents were depending on her, as were the children, despite their thanklessness. When she got home – then – maybe she would find every trace of the poor girl and place it, neatly, orderly, lovingly, into her room, before sealing it off. Return there no more.

The second room of her small bungalow to be sealed off and forgotten. Her daughter's room was kept just as it was too, the same as the day she left for the city.

Mrs Barcroft refused to think about it, passing the room each day without comment. As the years went by, the rooms grew fewer. With each her world becoming smaller. It was only natural.

Her legs trembled, but they'd carry her to the kitchen. She tried not to think of the young boys who'd done this to her, to her family. She tried not to think of her daughter as she was with them. How long had it gone on? When she'd called her yesterday to break the bad news it was a man's voice that answered. It was a man who she'd heard consoling her daughter as her daughter had started to scream.

Life was hard, she thought, as she clicked on the coffee machine. She pulled back the chair and sat down, watching the garden. She felt the plastic of the tablecloth gripping her fingers as she drummed lightly on its surface.

Then, on the frozen feeder, a robin. Its red breast flickered to and fro, tail wagged. Its round little head sinking between its shoulders and heaving a peanut through the mesh.

Breakfast in mouth, it flew to the top of the shed.

Mrs Barcroft's head sank into her hand. Ah, the shed. Her husband's shed. Another shrine to the dead. Another room off limits.

'At this rate I shall soon be homeless,' she said, grimly.

She pictured herself as a skeleton sat in her garden, the house transforming into one large tombstone.

She blinked the dreamy image from her eyes. It threatened to set her off. Exhausted, confused, bereft; she would start laughing hysterically and maybe never stop. And that would be the end of it.

The robin was gone. The garden bare. The first beams of light landed on the frozen pond and skidded across its surface, losing themselves in the snow-tipped grass.

The doorbell rang.

She jumped, startled and raised her head. Eyes suddenly open and twitching as they listened.

It rang again. Then again; two, three impatient times.

'Oh God,' Mrs Barcroft sagged. 'I should've known.'

A voice came from beyond the door. A woman's angry, yelling.

'Let me in! Where are you? I know you're there!'

A fist hammered weakly on the UPVC.

Mrs Barcroft stood, took a second to control her breathing. The hammering kept going. She steeled her resolve, strode to the door, and opened it.

Chapter Fifteen

Jen Barcroft

'I knew it!' Jen staggered.

'Jen,' her mother's eyes narrowed. 'You're drunk.'

'So?' she shook her head. 'I don't care.'

'It's not even seven o'clock. You'll wake the neighbours.'

'*I don't care!*'

Jen stumbled, leaning against the door frame.

'Where is she?' she asked, eyes wide. 'Where's Tasha?'

'Where?' Her mother said, shocked. 'You think she's here?'

'You've got her! I know it!'

'For God's sake, Jen. Come inside!'

Her mother dragged her drunken daughter into the hall and pulled the door closed behind them.

It was the first time in nearly a decade they'd seen one another. Tasha's seventh birthday. The visit lasted an hour before an argument had broken out. Tasha hadn't recognised her mother and Jen had accused Mrs Barcroft of turning the girl against her.

The truth was Jen Barcroft had run away from home at fifteen. The next her mother had seen of her was the day after her seventeenth birthday, when she'd returned home to leave the new-born Tasha with her grandma.

After that, Jen phoned three or four times. Then, nothing.

Her mother had kept the girl's room exactly how it was. Tasha's room would stay that way doubtless now too.

Mrs Barcroft lived in the cruel hope of Jen returning one day, sober and respectable. Jen, wearing a suit and black shoes, would walk through the door, hug her mother, and thank her for keeping her things just as they were.

As she stumbled now into the living room and slopped drunkenly down onto the sofa, Mrs Barcroft appeared to forget that dream.

'I've been up all night,' Jen began, sprawled out on the sofa the drink weighing heavy, lips sagging and consonants switching places.

'We've all been up, Jen,' her mother said. 'You're not the only one that's hurting right now.'

'Oh,' Jen shook her head menacingly. 'Don't pretend you're the only one here who cares about my daughter. She's *my* daughter!'

Her mother remained standing.

'Nobody's saying she's not, Jen. But we all have a right to be sad. To see Tasha snatched away from us in the prime...' a lump caught in her throat. 'In the prime of her young life... Well, it's a tragedy that doesn't bear thinking about.'

'Prime.'

As Jen said the word a baffled look crept across her features. To think of her daughter as anything but her daughter, young and dressed in pigtails, troubled her.

In her years in Manchester, Jen had taken to thinking of her daughter as she'd last seen her. Tasha, for her, was forever a seven-year-old. When the dawn broke on after-parties and the gin was making her teary, she'd take Tasha's picture out of her wallet and pass it around the room.

'*That's my daughter!*' she'd say. Her chest swelled with pride as her cheeks grew wet with tears. '*My daughter, that is! She's a star!*'

'Why've you got my photo up there?' Jen said, pointing to the mantelpiece. 'And who's that next to me? Is that me?'

'That's Tasha.' Mrs Barcroft said softly, knowing the response.

Jen's face flashed; a rictus of rage.

'You think I don't know my own daughter? You think I can't fucking tell the difference between my school photos and hers?'

'You're drunk. Perhaps your eyes are blurry.'

Her mother offered her a way out, before digging in her heel.

'Have you been drinking all night, Jen?'

'None of your business.'

'How did you get here?' She straightened her back, lifted her nose high in the air. 'Did you drive here like that? Or did one of your boyfriends drop you off?'

Jen folded her arms and looked away.

'You'd think this family had had enough trouble with men,' her mother said, lost now in exhaustion and fraying nerves.

'I thought you were a fluke, Jen. I admit it. Perhaps it was losing your father that did it? Perhaps you were unlucky? But now there's… another one of you gone. I have to wonder if it's in the blood.'

'You dried up old cow.' Jen snorted.

'You think just because you don't have any feelings, that the rest of us don't either? Well, guess what, we can and we do! You were a fucking horrible mum. Look how clean this house is!'

'How dare you.' Her mother began but her heart wasn't in it.

'That's your problem as well,' Jen sneered. '"*How dare you*" this and "*after all I've done for you*" that – it's like you want everyone to worship you. "*Oh, thanks mum, oh thanks!*" like that!'

Mrs Barcroft shook her head and spoke quietly.

'I don't think there's anything wrong with a mother expecting a little gratitude. A little respect.'

'What about love?' Jen stared up at her mother.

'Did you even think about that? Between all the cleaning up and the pleases and thankyous?'

'Of course, I did. I love you both. Deeply.'

'Really?' Jen turned away.

'Well you've a funny way of showing it.'

The room was silent.

Mrs Barcroft thought about offering Jen a cup of tea. But then, seeing her sat there, pouting, she thought better of it. She'd made it clear that she wanted no handouts in this life.

Her daughter was dead.

Jen felt her bare legs rubbing against the sofa. Hard cushions; square, with thick patterns. There was never any comfort in this house. No softness whatsoever. Jen blamed this on her mother. She imagined that her dad would have wanted things differently

She'd never met her dad. By all accounts, he was even more rigid than her mother. A disciplinarian. A stern man attributed to his high place in the town.

A stern man whose sternness is rewarded does not long for soft chairs. Still, Jen preferred to blame her mother.

Jen had been driven up to Avon Murray by her dealer, Devvo. He was the only man she knew who had a car and would give lifts without wanting something in return. Of course, what he really wanted was for her to keep buying his coke. She'd been coming back long enough that they were almost friends. He wanted to keep it that way.

They'd come straight from a party. She wore a skirt under the big coat Baz had lent her. Her mother's house was always cold. Colder now that the snow was deep. Still, Jen refused to shiver. The alcohol kept her warm.

'So, where were you?' Jen finally said, breaking the silence.

'Where?'

'When it happened? When Tasha was out with this boy who fuckin… you know.'

'Where was I?' Her mother stared vacantly.

'Is there an echo in here?'

Jen swung her boots down off the sofa and sat

upright. Her mother swayed like a ghost. The silence had brought their loss back into the room. It clung on to every surface, trembling on her mother's lip.

'I don't know.' Mrs Barcroft finally admitted. 'I don't even know. I'm sorry.'

'Sorry?' Jen looked puzzled.

A look of despair swept over her mother. Her lower lip upturned. Her eyes, normally so fixed and glowering, melted at the corners.

'She'd started going to her friends' houses after school. When I found out that one of those friends was *him*, the boy, it was too late to do anything. She'd been going out with him for ages, she said. She said she loved him, even. Silly girl.'

Jen remembered her first love. She doubted her mother remembered hers.

'Before I knew it she was arranging sleepovers. Sometimes with her friends. Sometimes with… him. I could never tell which one was which. She never told me. Just said she was going out.'

Jen placed her hands on her bare knees. Her mother's low voice in the early morning air gave her a chill.

'Then, one night, she went out. She stayed at someone's, I think. Maybe his place. Maybe her friends. Maybe she had an argument with him, or met a new boy? I don't know. She didn't come back.

'She'd been away for three days when I phoned the police. They said they couldn't do anything. Not unless I was certain that she was lost in the snow storm.

That was all they cared about. All they wanted to hear was that she was inside a house somewhere. It didn't matter which house, or who she was with, or whether I, her legal guardian, even knew where she was. As long as I thought she was inside then, they said, it would wait until after the freeze. It would wait, they said. She would be safer, they told me, wherever she was, than she would be if she was outside, trying to get home.

'Lots of people, they said, were trapped.'

Jen stared up at the mantelpiece as her mother spoke. Tasha, older, nearly seventeen. She looked like Jen. Perhaps one day, long ago, her mother too had looked like this.

'But she wasn't safe,' her mother swallowed. 'I knew she wasn't. I don't know how. Something inside told me. So, I planned. I thought, well, if the schools are open then that must mean that the emergency is over. Surely, if the children are returning to school, then that means it's all okay? The snow was light now. The houses further down the valley were unfreezing. In a week, or even a few days, people would be back out. Why not just declare it over now?'

Jen turned to her mother. 'What are you saying?'

'I'm saying that I opened the school up again. Three days ago. I went in, turned on the heating. I called all the staff. I said, anyone who can make it in, you come in. The rest could stay at home. Then, with everything coming back to life, I called the parents. All of you, I said, are welcome to send in your children. All of you.'

'What happened?' Jen asked.

'Not one mentioned Tasha,' Mrs Barcroft shook her head. 'Even that blowhard William Farringdon, the boy's father. He told me they were frozen in. He said the boy wouldn't be going anywhere. Well I saw that boy, Lucas Farringdon; the one that did it. I saw him in school on the very same day that they found the body. I saw him laughing. Bragging about it!'

Jen shook her head vigorously, her hands jammed over her ears. She didn't want to hear this. Not now.

Then, shoving her mother aside, she ran to the bathroom and started throwing up.

Chapter Sixteen

Mrs Barcroft

Mrs Barcroft stood, silent. She saw the yellow light of the morning turning to blue. It drained through the lace curtain like water through a colander, forming pools on the living room floor.

Perhaps she'd been too cruel. Perhaps there had been room for allowances that in the end she could never make. But she'd already lost one girl to a hard-modern world. To lose another...

No parent would take a risk like that. They knew where permissiveness lead.

And yet, the sight of her daughter had shaken her. Perhaps it was the aftermath of the loss? The shockwave had knocked loose her usual supports. The foundations of her world shifting, coming undone.

Not knowing why, she went in to the kitchen. She finished her coffee, washed out the mug, and went to the biscuit tin and opened it. Inside were a few hundred copper pennies; her change jar. She lifted it down onto the kitchen counter and rifled through it.

Right down at the bottom, she found a key. She lifted

it up to the light. *Yes*, it was the right one. She sealed up the change tin, put it back on the shelf, and carried the key through to the living room. She sat it, pride of place, in the centre of the coffee table.

It was the key to the liquor cabinet. It hadn't been opened since Jen had left. She'd promised that day that she'd never touch another drop. No sherries at Christmas. No glass of wine on Friday night. She, and Tasha with her, would make up for with abstinence what Jen drank in excess.

Mrs Barcroft had placed the key on the table hoping that Jen would find it.

She couldn't tell why she did it. Perhaps it was a change of heart? A softening, after all these years. Or perhaps it was an act of spite? Either way; let her daughter drink. Let her drink her fill. She'd never drink away Tasha. The work of loss had already been done.

Jen staggered back into the room now, rubbing her mouth with a sleeve.

'So, are you going to school?' she asked her mother. 'You look dressed up.'

'I am,' Mrs Barcroft nodded. 'The children need to be cared for. No matter what happens to me and my family, I must uphold my responsibilities.'

'You're a fucking martyr,' Jen said, collapsing on the sofa again.

Her voice had changed now. She rolled her eyes. Anger replaced by a petulant humour. She noticed the coffee table, and the key which sat in the middle.

'So, you're going to the school?' Jen confirmed.

Mrs Barcroft nodded.

'Where's Tasha?' Jen asked, her eyes fixed now on the key. 'Where's her body?'

'I told you,' Mrs Barcroft swallowed. 'They can't get her out. She's in the river.'

'I know!' Jen shouted. 'Which river? Which one!?'

'I don't-'

'You do! You know where she is! Don't lie!'

'I'm sorry, Jen.' Mrs Barcroft shook her head. 'I don't know why I didn't want to tell you... It's up in the valley. One of the pools. The one with the footbridge at its base. In the forest. Where the water opens up. Just...'

'Just what?'

'Just promise me you won't go. Not now. Sleep first. Rest. Prepare yourself.'

Jen swallowed. Her lips were dry, mouth cracked, saliva thick in her throat.

'I'm not promising anything,' she said. 'You go to work. The children need you.'

Mrs Barcroft looked down at her daughter. The girl who'd once been so full of life was now a shrunken, dark-eyed mass huddled there on her sofa.

She hated to leave Jen alone but, as Mrs Barcroft told herself, she must. Jen had made her choice long ago. She didn't want her mother any more. So be it.

'Alright,' Mrs Barcroft nodded. 'There's food in the fridge. Your room's how you left it. Get some rest.'

* * *

Jen nodded and kept staring, unfocused, at the flat expanse of coffee table.

She heard Mrs Barcroft leave, heard the door click shut behind her and the tip-tap-tap of her heels down the path.

Her mother went away. Jen didn't reach for the key. Not immediately.

Five minutes passed. Five minutes of nothingness. Five minutes of rest and silence. Five minutes of her breath echoing, deafening her in her own head. Then she reached for the key.

Her mother wasn't much of a drinker. She never drank more than two glasses of anything. As a result, many of the bottles she kept were top shelf; sherries and whiskeys, ports and gins. Things that would keep.

Jen normally avoided spirits. She got too drunk too fast. Cider and beer, maybe white wine, were enough for her. Things she could sip at all day and never black out.

The collision of Jen, her grief, and Mrs Barcroft's liquor cabinet produced a predictable result. Drunk and wild with despair, Jen had wandered out into the snowy streets with a bottle in her hand. She hadn't seen her daughter's body. She demanded to see it. She stumbled down the streets, jabbering to herself one moment, screaming and balling the next, sobbing, then hurrying silently towards the crime scene. She refused to sober up, despite the cold slap of wind.

The body had driven her mad. Afterwards she could not even remember it.

She couldn't remember her daughter's red hair, nor the red of her shattered nails as they splintered on the ice with her scratching.

She wandered then, afterwards, around the town she had done everything to forget. Memories came back to her. Boy's houses. Girl's houses. Teacher's houses where she'd thrown eggs in some far past. She held the gin bottle close to her and moved on, blown in strange directions by the wandering wind.

A layer of skin came off her knees as she scrambled on the ice. These bled now. Red droplets ran in crooked trails down bare flesh. Ice crystals hung in her coat and hair.

The weather got worse. She didn't know where she was going. She felt like she was being moved with purpose, but a purpose she didn't understand. The wind knew. The storm carried her.

Chapter Seventeen

Lucas Farringdon

It had been a day since the body was discovered. For the gossips of Avon Murray, it was a busy day indeed.

Due to the snow, much of their work was done on the phone. Still, there were whispers in the supermarket. Idle chats by the petrol pumps. Huddles in the pubs. Everyone had their own opinion. Everyone had a theory.

Almost all of them pointed to Lucas Farringdon. Word of the arrest had come out, but even before that there was sufficient evidence for people to start talking. The boy had been seen with the girl. The boy's father, they said, was rich. This was enough.

When Lucas was released without charge, his guilt, for the gossips, was absolutely confirmed. The rich get richer, they told each other. There's one rule for them, another for us. One mouthed a truism, and the rest nodded sagely.

William Farringdon knew what was happening. He'd been around long enough to know the way people are. He tried to speak to his son, to convince him that he shouldn't return to school.

'But if I don't go back, they'll think I'm guilty!'

'No matter what you do now,' William said grimly. 'They'll find a way to paint you as a criminal. If you go out they'll call you heartless. If you stay in, they'll say you're hiding. Best to avoid the buggers altogether.'

'No, Dad.' Lucas' mind was set. 'I'm sorry, but I have to go in.'

So, William was left behind, ruminating by the fireside, Scout huddled at his feet, while his son ran the gauntlet of public opinion.

His first test came on the approach to the school gates.

As the snow loosened, children flooded in to the school. After two weeks home schooling, parents were yearning to breathe again. Children hiked in, wading through snow, sometimes up to their middles, carrying all their books and pens, their lunchboxes and, in their crooked little hearts, the pure joy of knowing that a pariah was in their midst.

Lucas called to his old friends. They turned their heads. Some even ran, full speed, in the opposite direction.

Meanwhile, the children that he didn't know now pointed at him. Some pointed when they thought he wasn't looking. Others pointed openly and enthusiastically.

'There he is!' one first year shouted out in excitement. 'There's the boy that did a murder!'

In class, no one would go near him. The seat beside him was always empty. When the teacher got to his name on the register she paused, looked him up and down, before reading it slowly and carefully: 'Lu-cas Farr-ing-don', like a lion trainer with an unbroken animal.

'Here,' he said. His hand up.

He raised his hand as he'd been taught to do and tried to answer the teacher's questions. He even smiled, certain his guiltlessness would win through.

There was chilly silence from the class. Silence followed by whispering, as those who lived further out of town were all notified of Lucas' crime. Word spread. It took a few seconds at the start of every class, but once the silence settled again, Lucas was sure they all knew.

'We were supposed to be working in pairs today,' one teacher said as her lesson began.

She stared down at Lucas and the wide berth that his classmates had given him. She'd decided that to assign another child to him may be to tar them with his shame. The black guilt of murder would stick to them as it had to him.

'It's okay though,' she said, reassuring the rest of the class. 'We can work individually. No-one will have to...'

She swallowed her last words.

Classes creaked on horribly. Minute after minute ticked past. The day felt unfathomably long.

It was with tremendous relief that a knock finally came on the glass door. It was a man Lucas didn't recognise with a not from the headteacher, Mrs Barcroft. She wanted to speak with Lucas.

'Absolutely!' the teacher beamed. Then, with an effort, she made her face solemn and called Lucas from his seat. 'You follow this man, Lucas. He'll take you where you need to go.'

'I know where Mrs Barcroft's office is.'

'Well, this man will make sure you get there okay.'

As the door slammed behind him, Lucas could hear the chattering. Only now, as he walked away from it, did he realise that this would be a story they'd tell, each of them in their own way, until the grave. The day a murderer was in their class. He could hear their accusations, their nasty jokes, filling his head. They rattled about in there.

He started breathing heavily as he mounted the stairs. There were seven flights to climb before Mrs Barcroft's office. He would stare out of each window during the ascent. He would watch the white sky. The constant blanket. He would shake his head and climb on.

Chapter Eighteen

Mrs Barcroft

Behind her desk, Mrs Barcroft finished another coffee.

She held the mug by its dainty handle and pursed her lips. The machine left grains in the bottom of the cup which caught in her teeth.

Three knocks, slow and steady, tolled upon the door.

She swallowed the coffee. *Was she really going to face him?* She'd called him to her office almost unconsciously. The reality of it hadn't faced her until now.

'Come in,' she said, setting aside the cup.

Lucas Farringdon walked in. The man who'd led him there shut the door behind them. It was just the two of them now.

'Well...' Mrs Barcroft began. 'I didn't expect to see you at school this morning, Lucas.'

'In fact, if I'm being totally honest,' she rubbed her lip as she spoke. 'I didn't expect to ever see you again. Not after... you know.'

Lucas stood silent.

'You aren't very talkative, are you Lucas?'

He looked down at his shoes. She sneered at the boy's

nonchalant face. Young. Blonde. Handsome in his way. He must've thought he was going to get away with it.

'You may've somehow fooled the police, Lucas, but you won't fool me.'

He raised his eyes then. She grinned, happy to have at last caught the boy's attention.

'Oh yes, I'm under no illusions as to where the blame lies regarding my granddaughter's death. I know that you've been seeing her. I know that she's been staying at your house. She might've told meotherwise, but I've been in the know all along.'

His eyes watered.

'So,' she gestured at the boy to speak. 'What do you say to that? What answer do you have?'

Lucas coughed, throat was full of saliva. Looking like he might drown. He was unable to speak.

'Hmm?' Mrs Barcroft prompted again.

Lucas swallowed.

'Mrs Barcroft. I loved Tasha-'He paused as he saw her face fall. '-I...'

He tried to continue, but he couldn't find the words. What more was there to say?

Mrs Barcroft began chewing. The way she did when agitated. Chewing over words that she knew she couldn't say.

'Are you sure, Lucas, that this is the line you want to take? I mean, if you really *loved* my granddaughter, would you be dragging her away from the safety of her home? To go carousing around with you?

'Would you encourage her to lie to her own family? To

hide your relationship?' She shook her head solemnly.

'These don't sound like the actions of someone in love, Lucas. These are the actions of someone with a very guilty conscience indeed.

'You realise, Lucas, that while you insist on your silence, my daughter is left without her own daughter's body? You realise that we cannot properly mourn? No funeral can be held. Everything is frozen over.'

Mrs Barcroft's upper lip wriggled. The double meaning had crept unintended into her words. She thought of the girl beneath the ice and she blinked, repeatedly, forcing away the tears.

Chapter Nineteen

Lucas Farringdon

He looked down at his shoes again.

In his mind, he was back in the interrogation room. He would say nothing. Offer nothing. Answer only direct questions and do so only with direct answers.

A thought ran through his mind. He was unable to shake it.

It seemed like every time he opened his mouth; the adults would swoop in and tie him up with their language. They could speak better than he could. They could wrap him up with their words. They could turn what he'd say against him; even when what he was saying was the truth.

They said he had bad intent. They went searching in undertones and never listened to the content of his words. Suspicion had made them deaf.

He would stay silent.

His dad had told him that this would pass. He hoped it would. But he couldn't help thinking that the adult world was a lying world.

And he did have guilt. This was true. But he was not guilty. With guilt in his heart, it was best to stay quiet.

'Our family, what little of it there is left, is owed some answers, Lucas. We can't wait for the autopsy. We can't wait for the snow to stop and the river to unfreeze. We need answers, and we need them now.'

Lucas remained silent, staring at his shoes.

Despite his great sadness and terror, guilt and shame, a smile began to crawl across his lips.

'Do you not understand, Lucas? We will have no resolution unless you admit it. Admit what happened. Tell us what it was that you did.'

His lips were burning, eyes creasing up. All of his body fought against it but, as he thought about it, about the very inappropriateness of it, his lips tightened. They tightened and tightened.

A smile crawled across them, slow and fuzzy – painful – like a toxic caterpillar.

'Are you…?'

Mrs Barcroft stared.

Lucas shook his head. He lifted his hands up and rubbed them on his lips. He couldn't stop it. It wouldn't stop.

'I'm sorry,' he said.

In his voice he heard the crackle of hysteria.

Mrs Barcroft looked at the boy as he smirked. She watched him as he held in his laughter.

'I'm sorry,' Lucas giggled. 'I'm so sorry. I don't know why it's happening!'

'Stop!'

Mrs Barcroft stood and slammed her fist down on the table. She pointed at him, shaking her finger in fury.

'Stop that! Right now! Do you hear? I won't have it!'

'I'm sorry,' Lucas laughed. 'I'm so sorry.'

His diaphragm spasmed, up and down, up and down. He was laughing. It was inside him, coming from deep down; massive laughter. Snot ran down from his nose. His throat rubbed raw. His lips burned and stinged, as they pulled back over shameful teeth.

He couldn't stop it. He was possessed.

'You monster!' Mrs Barcroft cried. 'How could you do this? You are worse than I thought! Worse than anything I could ever imagine!'

Mad with grief, she picked up her coffee cup and threw it across the room. It missed Lucas' head by inches, smashing against the door.

At the sound of smashing, the man who had led Lucas up to Mrs Barcroft's office leant in.

He saw the boy. His slender young body was doubled up with laughter. His mop of blonde hair hopped up and down on his head. Mrs Barcroft's face was crimson, her eyes streamed water and mascara. She was yelling and screaming.

The man grabbed Lucas by the arm and yanked him out of the office.

'Ow!' Lucas cried.

He snapped immediately out of his hysteria.

'No!' Mrs Barcroft shouted after them. 'Don't hurt him! Don't make him a martyr! He is evil, hear me! Evil!'

The shock of Mrs Barcroft's screaming loosened the man's grip. Lucas broke free.

As the man turned, Lucas was already running away down the stairs. For a moment he leapt to chase the boy but then, hearing the headteacher's wails. He had to comfort the grieving head, even if it meant letting the boy escape.

But Lucas didn't escape. He didn't even leave the school grounds.

Instead, he went to the bike sheds. He strode there, head downturned, hands in pockets. He made himself small as he tramped the corridors and then out, across the grounds, to the place where he'd once tried smoking, and not liked it, then had his first kiss, and not liked it much either. The bike sheds were where, only days ago, locked in a frozen house, he'd really longed to be. Back there again, with his friends.

His friends, it seemed, were no friends now. They, like the rest, were suspicious. The black tar of murder clung to him so thickly that even his closest buddies, even those who had always stayed close to him, admired him, wanted to be him; were all his enemies now. They shunned him. Whispered about him behind his back. The braver ones said it to his face.

He would duck behind the bike sheds and wait there until lunch.

What he'd do at lunch he didn't know. Hang around like a ghoul, he supposed. Like the ghost of his former self.

But when he did reach the bike sheds, he wasn't the only one there.

'Oh, hey,' a girl said.

She wore a long black hoody, thick eyeliner, dyed black

hair. A goth girl. He recognised her from one of his science classes.

'Hi,' Lucas said back, pathetically.

She blushed a little.

'Are you hiding too?'

He nodded.

They stood in silence for a moment.

'I just got called to Mrs Barcroft's office.' Lucas grinned sheepishly, pointing back at the school with his thumb.

'I laughed in her face. I shouldn't have but, I don't know... I couldn't help it I guess.'

'You laughed?'

The girl's eyes widened.

Lucas smiled at her. He remembered her now. He liked her face, the way she jumped out of her skin every time you talked to her.

'You're Frigg, right?' he nodded. 'We had science together.'

She nodded too.

'Chemistry.'

Lucas slammed his back against the corrugated iron of the bike shed. He sighed deeply, feeling the tension of the morning pooling in his extremities.

Frigg made to say something, then didn't. Instead, she took a pouch of tobacco out of her pocket and rolled up.

'You want one?' she asked, not looking at him.

Lucas brushed his fringe out of his eyes. He sniffed the air as she sparked up.

'You know what,' he said. 'You're alright. I don't feel like it.'

'Scared?' she smiled.

'Of cancer? A bit, yeah. Or do you mean about getting caught?'

'Both.'

Frigg sucked a big cloud into her lungs and blew it out her nose.

'Are you scared of getting caught?' she asked.

The boy pushed back his blonde hair. He put a hand to his eyes, rubbing them.

Almost afraid to ask, so sick was he with the   constant guilt and blame. Still, he had to.

'You think I did it?' he asked.

She looked at him. Her dark eyeshadow had run in small smudges down the sides of her nose. Was her nose too long, he wondered, or was it just the effect of the black lines?

She turned her big eyes to the cigarette in her hand, away from his own.

'I didn't,' he said. 'Do it, I mean. If that's what you're thinking.'

'No?'

'No.'

He shook his head vigorously.

They stood in silence as she smoked the last of her cigarette. As it reached its end the paper came loose, spilling its contents down her hoody. She patted them off, dropped the filter to the floor and trod on it.

'I know you didn't do it,' she said.

'Really? How? Everyone's so confident that I did it. They all agree that I did it, even though I didn't. At least,

I think I didn't. But then, if I didn't, why do I feel so guilty about it? Why do I feel like I'm responsible, even when I know that I'm not?'

He was flustered. She liked him when he was like this. It reminded her of class.

'I know you didn't do it,' she repeated. 'Because I did.'

Lucas stopped in the middle of his self-recriminations. He looked at the girl. Frigg, her big eyes downturned and dark. She looked too pathetic to ever be a danger to anyone. There was no way she could harm Tasha Barcroft.

Lucas looked at the girl's awkward, lanky body and decided, without further question, that whatever she meant by her expression of guilt, it couldn't have been literal.

'Maybe we're all guilty,' Lucas said.

Frigg shook her head.

'Me more than others.'

'More than me?' Lucas asked.

She watched a grin spread across the boy's face. An evil sort of grin. A giddy one, mad, that he couldn't hold in.

Her tummy turned to see it. She grinned too.

'Well, maybe we're the same,' she said.

'Maybe the same,' Lucas laughed. 'Maybe we *are*! Both of us! Guilty as sin! Bonnie and Clyde!'

The goth girl smiled.

'Hey… I don't know what I'm doing here. I don't think it's doing any good being at school. It's like my dad said; they'll always find a way to get at you. You're damned if you do, damned if you don't.'

'Your dad said that?'

'Yeah.'

'That's pretty dark.'

'Well in this case I think it's true. I can't see the rest of the school day going any better than this morning did. And this morning was terrible.'

He checked his watch. There was still twenty minutes before the lunch bell would ring. If he was going to go he'd better do it now, before everyone could watch him leave.

'I'm gonna go,' he said.

'Oh.'

Frigg placed her hands in her hoody pockets.

Lucas looked at her. He couldn't be seen with her really. She'd be tarred with the murder brush too. Still, the thought of walking home alone, through the dead snow, through the angry little streets, it terrified him.

'You wanna come with me?' he asked.

Frigg nodded. She leaned down and picked up her backpack and pulled her hood up over her head. Lucas pulled his backpack on too.

As he walked, he felt her beside him.

Like a spectre she followed him over the playing fields, around the school building, up past the car park and away, out of the school, and on through Avon Murray.

Chapter Twenty

Inspector Todor

'They're okay I guess. The blood's flowing at least. That's more than can be said for Megan.'

'Megan?'

'Kivilahti, sir.'

'Oh yes,' the Inspector nodded. 'Of course.'

He was sat by the officer's bedside. The man he'd ordered on to the ice.

It was only yesterday, but it felt a lifetime ago to him.

For the officer too, time must have passed slowly. The man had been in and out of surgery all night, after all.

'The impact of the frozen water, well... it was like sticking your legs in a deep-fat fryer, they say.'

The officer sniffed. He didn't look the Inspector in the eye.

'Bursts a lot of capillaries. The skin comes loose. Later detaches. The pain's pretty horrible sir, I have to say.'

Todor nodded. There wasn't much else he could do.

He sat in the smelly chair the nurse had provided. The get well soon card he'd brought was on the bedside table. It was next to another, much bigger one, which had been signed by the rest of the station.

Todor hadn't been told about that card. He'd certainly not been asked to sign it. He made every effort to avoid reading what was inside. Whether they insulted him openly, or only by implication, he didn't want to know.

'Of course, they've got my bleeding under control now,' the officer continued. 'The very fact that there was bleeding was a good sign, apparently. Once you go into full shock the body focuses all its efforts on preserving the core. Megan, you see, she went in to full shock. They're having a hell of a time getting the blood to flow again, they say.'

Todor was silent.

The hospital was ten miles from Avon Murray. If he hadn't had a badge, he would've been stopped and turned back at five different roadblocks along the way. The big freeze had shifted keystones in bridges, made fords impassable, and had broken up the tarmac all along the high road. The official government guidance advised everyone to stay indoors.

The Inspector sighed and rubbed his eyes, exhausted. He struggled to contain his emotions. One moment the world was conspiring against him. The next it was all his fault. He was incompetent. The world was right to conspire.

His doubt pooled in the front of his brain. He could barely even think about the murder now. He could only think about his mistakes.

'They say I'll be up and walking in a week,' the officer smiled, grimly.

He clearly wanted to throw the Inspector a morsel of

sympathy, but Todor wasn't having it.

'It looked safe,' Todor said. His head in his hands.

The officer adjusted his collar.

'Yes, sir.'

'It did.'

Todor groaned into his palms.

'It looked safe. I mean, didn't it? Did it look safe to you?'

'It...' the officer furrowed his brow.

'Did it?'

'If I may speak candidly, sir-'

The officer swallowed as Todor lifted his blotched-red face.

'The guidance does recommend that you don't go out onto the ice. "No matter how safe it looks," it says. If I remember correctly.'

Todor's head plunged back down.

'In your defence, sir,' the officer continued through gritted teeth. 'If someone were in trouble I wouldn't think twice about it. I'd disobey the guidance every time.'

'Really?'

'Yes, sir,' the officer nodded. 'If someone were in trouble.'

Inspector Todor looked sheepish.

It had looked safe. He swore it had. If it wasn't thick enough to hold an officer then how was it thick enough to suspend the murdered girl? How could she hang there, frozen in time, her red hair splaying out as if caught in a cool breeze?

Liquid nitrogen, the mortician had said. Instant freezing.

'Sir.'

The officer nodded at the Inspector's coat. It was hung on a rack by the door. As Todor looked at the injured officer and then back at his coat he began to hear the chirruping. He was getting a call.

'Excuse me,' he said, scrambling across the room.

He dove out of the ward, his phone to his ear. A passing nurse rolled her eyes. Phones were, after all, meant to be switched off.

'Dafydd Todor here,' he answered. 'Who's this?'

'Is that you Inspector? We've been trying your radio for the past twenty minutes. Why weren't you answering?'

'Oh,' Todor scratched his head. 'I left it in the car.'

After a moment of hesitation on the other end, the voice of the dispatcher continued.

'There have been disturbances reported at the murder scene, Inspector. As acting investigator, the officers were requesting guidance from you.'

'What?'

He strode down a corridor. Then another, and another. He'd been looking for a mobile-friendly area, now he realised he was lost.

'What's happened?'

'Would you like me to summarise the reports?'

'Yes please.'

Seeing a door, the Inspector barged through it, the phone still lodged to his ear. He found himself in the children's ward. A nurse, seeing the baffled look on the Inspector's face, shooed him out.

'The first report concerns a couple of persistent

onlookers. One is female, dressed in dark clothes, around school age. The other is the initial suspect identified as one Todd Morrow. Officers report that they have been hanging around the body a lot. They were there late into last night, with the female returning in the early hours of this morning. She spent just under three hours with the body, leaving at 8:30am.

'The second report is marked urgent, and regards a female, scantily clad, in her thirties, who reports that she's the victim's mother. She was visibly intoxicated and demanded to see the body. Upon seeing it, she became distraught and then violent. After an officer made an attempt to restrain her, she scratched him quite badly in the face. She then made her escape.

'They say she got out onto the ice, sir. That she was clawing at it. Trying to get to the body. The officers were afraid that she would fall in.'

Inspector Todor scratched at his head. So, it had been thick enough to hold her...

'And where is she now?' Todor asked. 'Have we dispatched any officers to bring her in?'

'For affray, sir? Or for drunk and disorderly?' the dispatcher asked.

Todor's eyes darted. He remembered the last arrest. The accusing eyes of the boy's father.

'Just for questioning,' he coughed. 'And for her own protection'.

'Yes, sir.'

The dispatcher could be heard tapping on her keyboard

on the other end of the line.

The Inspector, thoroughly lost, walked past a cafeteria. He gave up looking for an exit. He pulled up a chair and sat, elbows on the table, listening for the dispatcher's response.

'I've checked the system, Inspector, and I'm afraid that there aren't enough free officers to conduct a   patrol.'

'Not enough officers?'

Todor shook his head in disbelief.

'How can there not be enough?'

'There has been a burglary report come through this morning, sir, and a case of mass truancy.'

'Truancy?'

'Six or seven children, sir. Four officers are required to bring them back to school. The burglary suspect is known to us and the remaining officers have been dispatched to bring him in.'

'So, who's left?'

'The officer posted to the crime scene, sir, and you.'

The Inspector swore under his breath. The woman behind the lunch counter gave him a dirty look.

'Okay!'

The Inspector made a snap decision. Too much had gone wrong already. He needed to take some risks, just some, if he were to get anywhere.

'Has there been any change in the victim's condition?'

The dispatcher sounded confused.

'Sir?'

'Has the body come loose? Is the ice melting?'

'Oh.'

He heard her switch to another line, mumble something and receive mumbling back.

'No, sir. The officer at the scene reports no change.'

'Okay, well we can be sure that the body isn't going anywhere. Tell the officer assigned to the scene that he… or she… whoever it is, should go and pursue the victim's mother. The scene can go unwatched for a short time. Meanwhile, I'll get in my car and head straight back over there.'

'When can we expect you back in Avon Murray, sir? So, I can report it to the duty officers?'

It had taken an hour to get there. Hopefully it would be quicker going back the other way, but Todor had little reason to believe it would.

'Just tell them I'm on my way,' he said. 'Over and out.'

With that, he hung up.

The second after he did so, he realised that he ought to have put out an APB.

'Damn it!' he swore again. Seeing the dinner lady about to yell at him, Todor strode away.

He would ask a nurse the way back to the officer's room. He would make his apologies. He would find a way out of this labyrinthine hospital, call in the APB from his car, and head back to the crime scene. With any hope, the situation would have improved by the time he got back.

Across the space of the next forty-two minutes – the time that it took him to get back to Avon Murray – the snow fell harder, the wind whistled through the freezing air and many residents of the small town turned their eyes to the heavens, expecting worse.

When the storm began, these sudden lashings of ice against their windows had heralded more days of snow and seclusion. Now that the storm was widely considered to be ending, the return of the ice winds came as a fatal omen. Perhaps it was coming back? Perhaps it would last forever?

On the streets of Avon Murray, the handful of officers left had difficult decisions to make. With their new and uncertain Inspector acting as CO, most officers were quietly neglecting to call in their encounters. Better to try and solve the cases there and then than entrust them to him.

Perhaps he would get better. They hoped so. But for now, with the danger of the weather, and perhaps a murderer on the loose, there was no time for uncertainty.

Staying off their radios, the officers of Avon Murray got more and more dispersed. Each pursued the small incidents happening right there in front of them. There was no attempt at any large-scale coordination.

Fallen chimney pots were picked up. Cats were rescued from trees and dogs from snowdrifts. A patrol car was parked across the main road, forming a makeshift pinch point, the better to slow traffic and conduct wary travellers.

What went untouched was the body of Tasha Barcroft.

It remained locked in the ice, as firmly as ever. The snow fell down over her like a veil. If officers were there they might have thought of erecting a tent – something to keep the snow off – but as the Inspector had sent the only officer assigned to the body off to do something else, no other member of the police felt able to visit the site either.

The APB, when it did come through, did very little to change these attitudes. Nobody rushed to search for the victim's mother. They simply kept on with whatever minor task they were currently performing, keeping an extra eye out in case a woman wild with mourning should pass them on the road.

As Inspector Todor nuzzled his car around the final roadblock, his car radio finally barked into life.

'Yes,' he answered. 'Inspector Todor here.'

'Inspector?' the dispatcher's voice was hesitant.

It was a different voice from the previous. He wondered what warnings had been passed over with the change of shift.

'Continue dispatcher,' Todor said. 'I'm approaching the town now. I can see the chimneys smoking.'

The dispatcher ignored the Welshman's touch of whimsy.

'A report has been called in, sir. From the undertaker's office. Mr Drąg's; the unit's pathologist.'

'Yes, I know Drang.'

'Mr Drąg called in a few moments ago, sir. He reports an assailant, female, who fits the description of Jen Barcroft. He says she turned up at his office, visibly intoxicated, angry and shouting. She is demanding to see her daughter and appears confused as to whether Mr Drąg has the body, or is able to get at the body, or where the body currently resides.'

Inspector Todor rubbed his chin.

'But only forty minutes ago I was told that this same woman was at the body itself? Down by the river?'

He turned up his windscreen wipers as the snow grew heavier.

'Scratching at the ice, they said...'

'Mr Drąg did report that she was confused, sir.'

'Indeed,' the Inspector nodded. 'Okay, dispatcher, could you please find me another officer? Two more, ideally. I am entering town from the South, which should put me at the undertakers within the next five minutes.'

'Yes, sir.'

The dispatcher could be heard tapping his keyboard.

'Any officers in particular, Inspector?'

Inspector Todor thought about different faces. He could think of no individual name; only composites, or nearby names that he'd remembered as pneumonic devices. The little tricks he'd developed to help him remember things were, he admitted to himself, more often than not, simply an additional set of obstacles he'd made for himself.

Had his memory always been so bad?

'Any particular officer, sir?' the dispatcher repeated.

Todor blinked and tapped on the wheel. No. None were coming.

'No, thank you,' he replied. 'Just whoever's free I suppose.'

'Nobody's free, sir.'

'Then whoever's closest, damnit!'

Todor slapped the wheel in frustration.

Then, as he turned the corner, the saw the scene in all its ugly unfolding. He made a last call.

'Sorry for the swearing, dispatch. Just send whoever's

closest. I'm arriving at the scene now.'

As he pulled up, Todor saw the unruffled Pole standing in the snow. His pipe puffed gently between his teeth.

Jen Barcroft, the victim's mother, was crouched in a shivering bundle. A dusting of white covered them both, suggesting that there had been very little movement for the past five minutes.

'Ah, Inspector,' Drąg said as Todor climbed out of the car. 'I am honoured to see you again. I had expected only a regular policeman. See my dear-'

He addressed the squatting woman, pointing at the Inspector with his pipe as he did so,

'They have sent out their highest-ranking officer to collect you. Is this not an honour?'

Jen was impervious to the situation. Past caring now and in a place where the world couldn't reach her.

Somewhere underneath her coat was the shape of a gin bottle. Other than the warm gin swirling around inside it, she was silent. Her body having reached near-total numbness.

The Inspector ran over to her.

Far from the clawing and screaming he'd expected, she seemed not to notice his approach. From what he could see of her appearance, she was worn ragged, totally exhausted.

She mumbled to herself, sounding like the same phrase on a loop.

'What's she saying?'

The Inspector turned to the pathologist.

He nibbled on his pipe, taking a long suck and blowing out a cloud of wet air.

'She's been saying "why can't you save her". "Why can't you save her?" Over and over.'

'Save her?'

The Inspector looked down at her. He could hear it now, just about. It crept out on her breath.

'A curious case,' the mortician said. 'At first I thought she wanted *me* to save her. I assume this is the girl beneath the ice she wants saving, yes? I wasn't sure at first, but then I remembered how small this town is. Two deaths in two days would be far too exciting.'

Todor looked down at the woman. She was rocking back and forth very slowly. She'd started shaking her head, as if denying everything.

'So, I said that I could not help the girl who is beneath the ice,' Drąg continued. 'For, as I told you previously Inspector, I believe her suspension in ice to be some form of supernatural occurrence. It is even, perhaps, a miracle.'

'You said this?' The Inspector asked. 'To her?'

Drąg shrugged his shoulders.

'It stopped her attacking me.'

'You shouldn't have said that,' the Inspector sighed. 'You can see what a state she's in. That kind of thing could push her over the edge.'

'What edge?' Drąg asked, contemptuously.

Then, his face softening, he tipped out his pipe.

'She kicked my dog, Inspector. I am an old man. She was very drunk. Still is, I don't doubt.'

'Nevertheless, she's in a delicate state. You shouldn't have put those ideas in her head.'

Just then, a siren came wailing down the drive. It was the back-up.

A man and a woman, heavy with cold-weather equipment, leapt out of the car and ran to Jen.

'And what about you?'

Drag replaced his pipe.

'Have such ideas entered your own head, Inspector? Do you believe in the supernatural? In the immaterial's active participation in the material?'

'Shall we get her in the car, sir?' officer Hanratty asked.

'Yes. But be careful with her. She's had a rough morning.'

'You have a lot of sympathy, Inspector.'

The pathologist said it loud as Todor walked away.

'Just be careful that this sympathy does not lead you astray. This is a matter of life and death, yes?

'Although,' he mumbled as he went back indoors. 'I suppose all matters are a matter of life and death. What else is there otherwise?'

Rosie was scratching at the inside of the door. As he went in, she ran out. Running onto the lawn, barking. She barked at the Inspector until the cars rounded the corner and climbed the hill to the station.

Chapter Twenty-One

Lucas Farringdon

'So, you were jealous of her?'

'I suppose I was. I think we all were.'

Lucas and Frigg walked the backstreets of Avon Murray. Their feet swung, slow and aimless. Their lips blew cloudy shapes in the cold.

'She really was something special.'

'I suppose,' Frigg said.

While he was lazy, warming his cockles on memories, she was trepidatious, like a hand reaching in to a dark hole.

'I thought everyone liked her?' Lucas said. 'She was popular, wasn't she? I mean, I probably shouldn't say it of myself, but I think I was too. Until now.'

'She was popular,' Frigg agreed.

Lucas turned to her. Her wide staring eyes had grown on him. Something about the thick black liner that surrounded them made her thoughts easy to read.

He'd always struggled to read Tasha's thoughts. Whenever they were together a strange aura leaked out of her. It made him dizzy. Unable to feel how he normally felt. His vision went all blurry. His thoughts were thick. One moment he would be thinking rationally, the next he'd lose all clarity. His sense of self, ultimately, would wash away.

He wondered now, in the presence of this eminently knowable girl, whether he'd ever really known Tasha Barcroft at all.

'Why are you so tense around the word 'popular'?'

'Me?' Her eyes grew wider. 'I'm not!'

'Yes, you are! You say it like it's a weird thing. Like you're saying one word and I'm saying another. Like it's only by coincidence that the two words sound the same.'

Frigg was angry. She liked the boy, it was true, but he so unaware. It was like he couldn't imagine anyone thinking otherwise than himself.

'When you say popular,' she started, pausing a moment to think about what she was asking. 'What exactly do you mean by the word?'

'Popular?'

Lucas laughed.

It was nice to talk about something that wasn't Tasha's death. He was beginning to enjoy it.

'Popular means that people liked her. Maybe not everyone, if what you say is true, but lots of people. Most folk got on with her... maybe? Is that what I mean? Either way, she had a lot of friends. People liked her.'

'Did they?'

Lucas looked at her, eyes narrowing, smile curling.

'Okay, go on then! What do *you* mean by popular?'

Frigg's hands trembled a little. She warmed them in the front pocket of her hoody, held against her belly.

'I guess I mean that... well, I've been thinking about it.'

'Yes? And what do you think?'

'I've been thinking about it. I think that maybe being popular doesn't mean more people like you, or that you've got more friends. Like, my friends seem to have as many friends as yours. I mean, I don't even really like people and I have more than a dozen friends. If, by friends, you mean people that you hang about with.'

'Right.'

Lucas was nodding. Frigg didn't think he was understanding. She kept talking, trying to ignore his smile.

'Well, Tasha doesn't... sorry, *didn't* seem to have any more friends than a normal girl at school. But she *was* popular. Everyone would agree that.'

'So...' Lucas scratched his head. 'So, you're saying that...'

He faded off. He still didn't get it.

'I guess maybe I'm saying it's quality not quantity... but, wait, no. That's not right.'

'No?'

'No. It's something else. Like, everyone knew Tasha. Girls wanted to be her, so were jealous of her. The boys wanted to be with her, and so were jealous of you. So, being popular, it didn't mean you had friends. It doesn't. If anything, it means more people are jealous of you. More people dislike you. Hate you even.'

'Then why be popular?' Lucas laughed. 'It sounds terrible!'

Frigg stared down at her Doc Martins.

'I was thinking the same thing.'

The two walked in silence a moment. Lucas ran his hand along a garden wall, scooping up the snow and, as he reached the wall's end, flung it up in the air. It hung there for a moment, drifting, before slapping down onto the ground.

'When we stop being in school, it'll all change,' Frigg said to the wind. 'What's popular. Who's popular. It'll all be different.'

'You think so?'

Lucas stared up into the sky.

'I hope so, actually. Life is boring, isn't it? I hate having everyone hate me. I should just do what my sister did.'

Frigg looked at him. She couldn't picture Luas Farringdon with a sister. She imagined a tall girl, handsome like him, wearing a dark dress and pearls.

'What did your sister do?'

'Went to Manchester.'

Frigg nodded.

Going to Manchester meant the end of Avon Murray life. Whatever fickle substance popularity was, none of it could cling to a body that had travelled to Manchester. The big city was spoken of very little, even by those whose friends or relatives or children had gone there. It was signified by a shake of the head, a hushed '*oh no, not for me that*', and general agreement that it was too noisy, too busy, and the people there were too rude.

London, by contrast, was pure hell. Even Mancunians agreed on that.

To have gone to Manchester meant the end of your life in the village. Even those who went to university there and returned only four or five years later were welcomed back like a sailor who's been long at sea. Immediate family were happy to greet them, but the rest smelt trouble on the wind. They always kept an eye on the citygoer. They wouldn't trust their children with them.

The Farringdons had come from the city. Lucas was not so naïve. He knew this helped with the rumours. For some, no doubt, it had only been a matter of time before children raised in the city committed some foul act.

Frigg, who travelled to Manchester in secret – shopping at Affleck's, going to gigs – felt the same taboo fog floating around herself. The looks she got.

Perhaps Lucas was right when he thought about leaving. Perhaps, it struck her then, she should leave too.

'What's the city like?' she asked. 'Does your sister like it?'

Lucas's face turned hard.

'I don't really want to talk about my sister.'

They walked on, silent.

'She doesn't speak to us, really,' Lucas said. 'And when she does it's always to cause an argument with dad.'

'She doesn't like your dad?'

'Sort of,' Lucas shrugged. 'I think she likes him. But she can't stand my mum. She argues with him about that.'

Lucas caught Frigg's eye.

'She drinks, you see. Mum does. Though probably Jo now too.'

'I'm sorry.' Frigg said.

The wind belted suddenly down the road. It hit them, hard. A gust shook icicles from the trees around them.

Frigg turned her back to the wind. Lucas held his face to it. He glowed with a quiet defiance. Clumps of snow slapped against his face and a white wetness clawed at him. He could feel his cheekbones and his nose. The outline of his visage - handsome, some said - Tasha said 'hot' – now hung in the air in front of him. Ice formed on his blonde fringe.

Lucas looked at Frigg. She looked back. They weighed each other for a second.

They were going to see the body, weren't they? Somehow, they just knew it.

'Are you guilty?' Frigg asked.

'Guilty? Why?'

Frigg shrugged.

'Why should I be guilty?'

Frigg turned towards the woods and began walking.

'I'm guilty,' she said. 'I can't shake it. I did it. I know that it was me. In my rational brain I keep telling myself I'm not to blame, but it doesn't work. It doesn't make me any less guilty. Even if I'm certain that I didn't do it, I still know that I did.'

She turned back to look at him.

'It's the guilt. You can't shake it.'

As she walked on to the woods, he followed. He followed because, if he didn't, he thought he might be sick.

'Okay,' he said, catching up to her. 'Maybe I am. A bit. But I didn't *do* anything!'

'It's okay,' she said. 'I don't know if anybody did, really. But we all did. Sometimes I think that everyone here is guilty. Everyone in this little town. Everyone in this country. Maybe everyone in the whole world.

'Then I think: maybe that's why we're so quick to judge. Maybe that's why we love other people's sins. We love reading about them. We can't get enough of other people's faults. Why? Because we're guilty. We know we are. We struggle with it every day. Often, we don't even know what we're guilty about, what we're sorry *for*. We didn't do anything! So, when someone comes along and gets caught for doing something; oh, then it's a fucking celebration. Then everyone gets the knives out. You did it! *You!* Not *me!* I didn't do *anything!* It's all *you, you, you!*'

Lucas' hands were cold, even in his pockets. Sleet fell now like a drumroll of little taps. They walked on into the sleet as it fell heavier than the snow.

'Do you think that's what it is?' he asked.

'I don't know. Feels like it to me.'

The road dropped down ahead of them. Across the valley he saw the Roundy hill. At the start of the storm he remembered children sledging there. Now it was abandoned. Frozen over. Dead as a gravestone.

The forest stood beneath it. Tasha's body somewhere inside. Flowers on her grave.

'I've never seen her, you know.'

Frigg turned to see his pale face, fringe over his eyes.

'Not since it happened,' he said.

They stopped walking as wind rattled down the road.

The crypt door opening.

Frigg leaned out and took Lucas' hand.

Lucas gripped it.

He felt the wind cold on the outside of his hand and the girl's warm fingers inside it. Something rattled in his heart. Like the girl, the boy didn't know quite what was happening, or why.

'Let's go,' Frigg said.

And, so they walked on.

The houses they walked past looked abandoned. Yet inside each was a cowering family, curtains drawn for warmth. Most would wait out the storm by the glow of the television. Some of the older residents lit their fires. Most of the younger ones turned to alcohol. Outside, every house was uniform; drawn curtains, lightless.

Nobody watched as the town's most hated boy was led by the hand along their frosty street. Nobody saw the goth girl as she slipped ever so slightly on the ice, or the arms of the boy that supported her when she nearly fell.

The ginnel where Inspector Todor first interviewed Lucas' father, was now unguarded. Blue and white police tape hung between the fence posts. Lucas and Frigg stepped over it and walked into the woods.

They stood among the twisted trees. It was calm there. Not silent – sudden gusts of wind could be heard, clattering windows and rustling leaves – but inside the forest, the angry howl was almost soothing.

They were out of the storm now and the snow which fell there only came in soft clumps. Airborne smatterings, drifting down from the leaves. Restful on the gathering white.

'It's all black and white,' Frigg smiled. 'Like a movie.'

'Have you been here before?'

She smiled.

'Yes. Have you?'

'Yes, but it was greener then. We went swimming here. In the pool at the bottom. We used to jump off the bridge.'

'That's where she is,' Frigg said.

They turned down the slope. The frozen pool barely visible from where they stood. They would have to descend further to get a good view.

Lucas held out his hand; the same way he'd done to Tasha, and, many years before, his mother. He found that, just like them, Frigg took it and held it, almost automatically. She led him on.

They scraped and scratched down the black and white path. Frigg tramped down the brambles with her Doc Martins. Lucas held her arm as she slid over a fallen trunk.

'Here.' She was pointing to the bridge.

They'd reached the valley floor.

'You can see her best from up here'.

There was blue and white tape there too. Smatterings of yellow and black intermingled with it. Two types of tape. Two warnings.

Lucas was reminded of the electricity substation he passed on the way to school, remembering its sign; *Danger of Death: Keep Out.*

Frigg was already standing on the bridge, looking down.

'You can still see her. She's getting covered over by the snow now, but she's still visible.'

Frigg turned back to Lucas.

'She hasn't moved,' she confirmed.

Then, with an ominous sweep of her arm, Frigg pointed out over the edge. In her black hoody she reminded Lucas of something else. Another image leapt unbidden to his mind.

'Come on,' she said. 'Look.'

Step by step he climbed the bridge and with shaking hands he took hold of its side. He leaned over. He looked.

For a moment, he just stared.

His face was hard. Stern. Angry, even. A single wet orb rose, like an egg, in the corner of his eye. Frigg turned away as it poured.

'I don't know why I came here,' he said. 'I don't know why I let you bring me. I didn't want to see. So, she's dead. So, what? You think I didn't believe it? That I wanted to make it real?'

He rubbed his fist on his trousers.

'It was real enough already, alright!'

'But-' Frigg began.

'I don't understand what you thought it would do,' he said. 'I don't know why I'm here. She's dead.'

The words struck him. He repeated them to himself.

'She's dead. She's dead. She's dead.'

Frigg pouted. She turned back to Tasha. The girl beneath the ice ignored them both. She was staring up at something far above them; up into the distant sky. There was something up there. Some beauty not visible to the unfrozen eye. Something far more interesting than them.

'She's happy,' Frigg said suddenly.

Lucas stared at her, then down at Tasha.

'I didn't make you come here,' Frigg said. 'You came yourself. You wanted to. I just led you. And, yes, I've come here before... I think, the more I stare at her – the more you do – the more we all do... the closer we get to seeing what she sees... maybe?'

'What?'

Lucas furrowed his brow. That science-class look of befuddlement.

'What are you talking about? You're sick.'

'The police never look at her,' Frigg said. 'They never look down. When they're here, guarding her, I mean. They just stare out at the horizon. They don't look at her because they know what I see. What we'd all see if we looked. If we all did...'

'You're crazy!'

Lucas shook his head. Screwed up his eyes. But in his eyes, he was pleading. All he'd seen was a corpse. The thing he loved, now lifeless. If only there was something more; something he wasn't seeing.

'Don't you see how beautiful she is?'

Frigg pointed. Lucas stared.

'I guess,' he said. 'But she was always beautiful.'

Frigg shook her head.

'No. Not like this.'

He wanted to see what Frigg saw.

The more he stared the less he saw Tasha. Her fingers clawing at the surface. That first sight of her was terrifying; a desperate and doomed scrabble for life.

As he looked closer, he saw that it wasn't panic that he saw on her features. She was locked in, frozen, preserved and totally still. A vision of absolute calm. Her arms and legs were like that of a bather, treading water in a warm pool. Her face was uplifted, and without a single crease. No effort. No pain. No sorrow.

In her eyes – Frigg was right – there was an undead and undying vision. It was still there. Something she'd seen, something eternal; it was clamped there by the ice.

'I see what you mean now. I think. I think I see it.'

'She's more now than she was then,' Frigg said.

She stood close to Lucas. Their two hands touched on the stone of the bridge.

'She's more than the girl who bullied me. More than your girlfriend. She isn't that girl anymore; the   popular one. She's something else.'

Their faces were close now. She turned to him.

'I wish everyone could see her,' Frigg said.

Then, his breath still shallow, Lucas kissed her.

She pulled back.

'I'm sorry,' Lucas said. 'I thought…'

'It's okay.'

Frigg shook her head and rubbed a little at her lips.

'This is all too much,' he said. 'I don't know what's happening.'

'I'm sorry,' Frigg repeated.

There was a moment of quiet as the snow fell softly on the ice. Two hearts beat loudly in two chests.

One heart was frozen solid, and its owner looked onward, upwards; away from this too-human scene.

Lucas looked at the goth girl. He noticed how she shivered. Her big, wide, downturned 'O's of eyes were black and white. Like the movies.

'I like you,' he said.

She swallowed.

He stared. In the silence, he repeated it.

'I like you, Frigg.'

She nodded.

'I'm glad,' she said eventually. 'But, well, I can't-'

'You can't?'

'I have a boyfriend,' she said.

Her fingers twisted in her pockets. Was this the first time she'd said it? Was it the first time she'd admitted the possibility, even to herself?

Lucas felt ice running down his spine. It carried on, right down his legs and out of his toes, like electricity.

'Who?' he asked.

'I can't say…'

He waited.

'Todd Morrow,' she nodded. 'I'm going out with Todd Morrow.'

Lucas frowned. His fringe fell in front of his eyes. He stared out from a yellow nest.

'The murderer?' he asked. 'The one who really did this?'

He pointed over the side of the bridge. He didn't look.

Like the police, he refused to look. He would only point.

She shook her head, breathing heavy now too.

'He's not a murderer!' Then, trembling. 'I'm the murderer. You are. We all are. We all killed her! We're all guilty!'

Lucas snorted.

'I have to go,' she said.

She turned away. Her hands, he saw, shook. Tears too, he didn't doubt. Unlike his own, but still tears.

He refused to stop her. He stood silent.

Instead he watched her drift away into the thickets. Saw her stumble over a patch of brambles. Saw her go. And then, instead of arguing any more, of fighting any more, of loving or of trying to think of love... he carried on over the bridge, up the other side of the valley. He followed the path that would take him home.

Chapter Twenty-Two

Frigg McBride

Todd's hovel was filled with ripe scents. The air was thick and smoky. Damp wood crackled in the fire as Todd and Frigg passed a slim white joint between them. Up above, the frozen chimneypot strained.

'It's cosy in here,' Frigg said.

She looked down at her fingers. They poked out of black fishnet gloves, pink like little frankfurters.

'It's good,' Todd nodded.

Frigg watched the ragged boy as he sucked on the joint and passed it to her. She liked his frail blonde whiskers. They coated his chin like a frost. She liked the layers of clothes he wore that made him look like a pile of discarded carrier bags.

'I wonder about you,' she said. 'You're so different. You live up here all alone. No family. No friends.'

She sucked on the joint and held it in, noticing she'd smoked it now right down to its ends.

'Sorry,' she coughed. 'You want this?'

He took the butt held it to his lips, sucking the last smoke out with tiny kisses.

'You never come down to the town,' Frigg thought aloud. 'But everyone knows you. They all talk about you. Especially now. *Todd Morrow! Todd Morrow!* It's like you're a celebrity or something.'

Todd threw the joint it into the fire, finally dead.

Frigg was sat opposite him. Since her first visit, Todd had rearranged his hut and made space for another person to sit. A space for Frigg, specifically, as he expected no other visitors.

'How did you end up out here?' she asked.

'I don't know.' He shrugged.

'You must know.'

He scratched at his smokedamp cap and thought.

The fire crackled and sparks leapt. Frigg watched him watch the flames.

'You must remember how you got here, surely?'

She narrowed her eyes, curious.

'Do you, Todd? Remember?'

Staring at the fire, he burped and wiped his lips.

'I guess I found it a few years ago, like I said. I don't like town. They made me the forest ranger. I got the hut because I look after the forest.'

Frigg rubbed at her ankle.

'I know about that, Todd. You've told me about that before.'

'Before?'

He paused, vacant, then threw another log on the fire. The wood was roughly hewn. His axe must've been blunt and his arms were weak with disuse.

'I guess I used to like the forest. When I was little, I mean. I liked the forest. We used to go playing out here, you know?'

'With friends?'

'Sometimes,' he coughed. 'Yeah, sometimes I came here with friends. Sometimes it was with my brother, like.'

'Your brother?'

Frigg never thought of him having a brother. She never thought of him having a family for that matter. He was a lost little boy, wasn't he? Like an orphan from the books.

'Oh yeah, my brother's great. He's away now. He went to America to sell cars. I told him he should just sell them here. People buy cars here. But he said he couldn't.'

'Why?'

'I don't know why.'

Frigg pulled her hoody up. It was still cold, even with the fire.

'We used to go for walks, me and my brother. He used to like going up the big hills. I preferred just walking in the forest. I didn't like the maps and the compasses, like he did. I didn't see the point.'

'You like getting lost.'

He furrowed his brow.

'I don't know. I don't think so. I just don't get why we couldn't just walk. Just be there in the trees, you know. Look at the animals. He was always wanting to run up to the top of every hill. He ran up there, like there was some big *prize* on the top or something. I didn't get it.'

'He knew everything, my brother. He knew the animals we'd see on the way. What all their names were, like. He even knew how long the walk would take. He'd be like, *oh this one's two hours*, and we'd set off and then, two hours later, we'd have got back to where we came from. I don't know how he knew all that.'

Frigg stretched her hoody over her knees.

'Maybe he read about the walks in a book?'

Todd blinked, looking angry. Or perhaps it was just the smoke getting in his eyes? He looked childish and resentful.

'I don't think he cheated,' he finally said. 'Didn't look in books or anything. He just knew.'

'Okay,' Frigg said. Then, after a moment of silence; 'He sounds like a smart guy.'

Todd nodded.

'Yeah, he was really smart. He got the girls too. All the girls liked him. When he took the girls home, I had to go out. I didn't really know where to go so I went to the woods.'

Frigg watched him. There was a sour tone in his voice. He still resented it.

'I liked the woods,' he said, unconvincingly. 'They were quiet. At home you could hear him and the girls going on and on and on about pointless crap. It's just bullshit, I told him. They're boring. *And* they always cheated on him.'

'Girls are bitches,' Frigg confirmed.

Todd was shocked.

'It's okay,' Frigg laughed. 'I hate girls as well. I don't know what guys see in them.'

Todd stared at her.

'Like Tasha?'

Frigg stared back. The sun had set, and in the flickering red light Todd looked malevolent. She knew that she, too, must look like the devil. She felt like the devil. The guilt ate her up.

She could feel the curse of her curses. Her black magic.

'Yes,' she said, her eyes wide. 'Like Tasha.'

'In fact,' she grinned darkly. 'Tasha was the biggest bitch of them all.'

Todd breathed heavily. He nestled down, deep into his mess of coats and shawls.

The girl had thick black lines of make-up around her eyes. She was like an ancient Egyptian, or a kind of old ghostly spirit. 'I used to go out to the forest all the time. I found this place when I was wandering about. I thought, maybe I should tell my brother and we can turn it into an awesome den. Then I thought, no.

'If I tell my brother then he'll just bring girls here and then that'll be two places I can't go. No den. No house. Nothing at all.'

'Maybe if you gave him the den then you could have the house?'

Todd shook his head.

'No. I like the forests.'

Frigg felt sorry for him. He trembled with the kind of guilt that she had inside too. Anxious energy. As she began to speak he interrupted her.

'I loved the forests! They were the only place where I could always go and it was always quiet and I might not have known all the trees and the animals and how long it would take to do walks but I knew about *some* things! I knew more than most people do-'

The words poured out of him at once.

'I know about what plants sting and what plants cure stings. I don't know what they're called but I can see them. I know what you can eat and what makes you sick. I know which mushrooms make you trip and where they grow and I know how to find the best ones and how to make tea out of them.

'I know all about the forests. More than the books do, or whoever writes the books.'

He was rocking now.

'And I would have been living out here already if it wasn't for the government. The government when they closed everything down and said nobody's allowed to go anywhere.'

'The government?'

'Yeah, and they put trays of blue chemicals and everybody who went near the forests and the fields had to splash their feet in them. And they rounded up a bunch of animals and next day there were big fires. You could see all the smoke and, when they burned a field of cows, you could smell it like a barbecue.'

Frigg stared at him. Then it clicked.

'Oh, you mean foot and mouth? Oh God, I'd totally

forgotten about that! I couldn't take the short cut to school because it went through a farmer's field. God, yeah! I remember that now!'

'I don't know what it was,' Todd said. 'But that's when they wouldn't let me come to the forest anymore. They said I couldn't come here-'

'-and the cows broke into the playground once,' Frigg remembered, talking over Todd. 'And, you're right, we came in the next day and there was all this smoke coming from near the cowsheds and it smelled of meat and, yeah, now I think about it, I don't think we ever saw any cows in that field again-'

'-so that's when I went to the city,' Todd said. 'And I did horrible things there. And it was all because I couldn't get back to the forest.'

His eyes glistened in the firelight. His face creasing up horribly.

'And if I'd just been allowed to stay in the forest then everything would have been alright. I didn't mean to do anything bad. I didn't want to hurt anyone!'

Frigg, who had been thinking about the poor cows, was surprised when she saw him crying.

'What...' she began. 'What did you do?'

He rubbed at his eyes with is sleeves. He shook his head. He wasn't telling.

He would remain silent.

Frigg watched him. Todd sat, silently rocking. Some old trouble was spilling down his face. Old trouble in search of new pity. She would give it to him, she was sure, if he would just talk.

But he wouldn't talk. She knew he wouldn't.

'You don't need to feel bad,' she told him. 'Whatever it was, I'm sure it's not your fault. You didn't even want to be in the city.'

'No,' he sputtered. 'No, I didn't.'

She felt pity for him. A rare type of pity; a type she'd felt very little of in her life. The type of pity that flushes the whole system with love. The type of pity that arouses.

She watched his pathetic face as it balled up, sobbing. She sensed his weakness. It was big and ugly in the small, cramped shack. It overwhelmed her. She felt for him, and felt that she wanted him.

'Don't worry,' she said.

She was up on her feet, too tall to stand straight in the hut. The air was thick with smoke when she stood.

'Don't worry,' she repeated, stepping over to him. 'Don't worry. Don't worry.'

He moved away from her, trying to hide his ashy wet face.

But she came to him. The tall girl wearing black, with her eyes, lined with black, soft now. She came to him and placed her arm around his shoulder and lowered herself down. She was around him now, wrapped around him in the cramped space, and he was around her.

'Don't worry,' she said from her lips. 'Don't worry. We've all done things we're ashamed of. We've all done bad things. Everyone is bad. Everyone is evil. Don't worry. Don't worry.'

His big shaggy head nodded and she pulled it down

onto her chest. It heaved there. She could smell the smoke and the sweat and the weed from his hat. His hair was wet with oil and melted snow.

'I've done bad things,' she said. 'I've done the worst thing you can do. I've killed someone. I have. Murder.'

He lifted his eyes from her chest. He looked up at her.

'I have,' she nodded. 'With magic. I've murdered someone with magic.'

He looked at her, mouth hanging loose.

'You know this,' she stroked his sticky head. 'I killed Tasha Barcroft. I murdered her with magic.'

The sticky head shook.

'It's true!' she whispered.

'She used to bully me. It's almost funny to think back on. It seems so unimportant now. You know, in contrast to what's happened. But she really did make my life horrible. Every morning I'd know what to expect on my way to school, and then after school I'd have to turn my phone off because that's when they came for me online.

'I don't even know if she meant it. She was like the leader, but she didn't tell them what to do. They just saw her lead and followed it. Maybe she didn't even care about me? She just saw that I was weird, that I didn't fit in. The rest would sense it and gang up. They'd leave posts. Nasty comments. Photoshopped pictures...'

She could feel his chest heaving. Perhaps he too had been bullied? Or maybe he was jealous of her, never having received that much attention. Perhaps, yes, like a ghost, he'd longed for any contact, even anger.

'I found a book,' Frigg said.

She stared into the fire as she thought about the book, its leathery case shimmering, the fire popped. Sparks crawled along the ground towards her.

'It was a book of spells and magic. I found it in an abandoned building I sometimes go to. One of those old prefab things, made of boards and stuff, from the sixties. It was all grown over with weeds. There were holes in the roof. It's probably fallen down now. After I found the book in there I never went back.'

The dark closed in. The snow creaked on the roof above them and they could sense the storm growing wilder outside. Huge clumps were coming down. Falling like they'd done in the worst days, right in the midst of the freeze.

'I read in there about the different spells. There was one. I can't remember its name. It was to bring harm to people. Cursing them. I don't know why I can't remember... it's like the spell itself is cursed. I can't even remember what the page looked like now. My mind... it's as if it's been wiped.

'I... I did the spell. As soon as I saw it I knew I had to do it. That it was the only way to get Tasha back for all the horrible things she'd done. The things her friends did. I knew that I needed to do it, I can't remember it now, and I remember the need. Like I was possessed.

'So, I went to the forest. Just here, really. Just up the river. Where the wildflowers grow, and the mushrooms.'

Todd nodded. He knew the spot. It was always damp in

the mornings and evenings, but got sun in the afternoon. It was where the magic mushrooms grew. The best ones.

'I picked some mushrooms, the ones from the pictures it had – why can't I remember them? – and then some purple flowers. There were certain roots I had to dig up, and then a bit of a newt. I had to catch it in the pool. The pool where she…'

Todd's eyes darted in the dark. The newts were rare. It hurt him to think of them injured, hurt, killed. It gave him a sadness in his heart. It made him restless, like he wanted to get up now and go rescue them, even though he knew they weren't there. All hiding now, they were. In the snow, they all hid. All the river animals.

'The last thing I needed. It's so gross to say…'

Frigg rubbed her hands together. She rubbed her fingers along her palms and down the backs of her hands, washing away invisible stains.

'I needed her blood, you see. That was the only way you could make the curse really stick. I needed to get her blood.'

'How did you get it?' he asked.

Frigg turned her face away from him. 'I'm not proud of it. It's really gross.'

'Okay.'

'I knew that when she refused to do P.E. it was because she had her period. There aren't enough women teachers for P.E. at our school so we're taught by Mr Rush. Everyone knows that Mr Rush hates hearing about periods. You say you've got a period and he lets you walk right off.

'I know,' Frigg suddenly grinned. 'Because I always have a period when P.E. is on.'

Todd Morrow's breathing was heavy. She could hear his heart thumping in his chest, mouth open. His breath passed through it, warm wind through brown teeth. Cloudy in the cold.

He didn't know what a period was.

'So, when she skipped P.E., I was skipping P.E. as well. I followed her. I don't think she saw me. Then, when she went into the toilet, I followed her there. I…

'I fished her tampon out of the disposal bin.

'I know, it's gross. I don't know why I did it. I was possessed, like I said. I took it out and that was the blood. *Her* blood. The blood that I needed.'

'How,' Todd asked. 'Did you know it was hers?'

'I knew it was hers because when I went to fish it out, it was still warm.'

Her face was rigid with remembered determination.

'And I took the ingredients out to the woods. Out to the old crying tree. You know, the one from long ago?'

He nodded. It was deep in the forest. Far away from everything.

'And I mixed the newt and the herbs and the flowers and the mushrooms and then some wine, taken from my mum, all in the same bowl. I said some words – I can't remember them now – and then I put in her blood and then, the last thing, I pricked my finger.'

'*Your* finger?'

'Yes,' she smiled now. 'The last ingredient was the blood

of a virgin. I know that Tasha's not a virgin. She is… *was* a slut. So, I needed more blood. So, I pricked my own finger.'

'So, you're…' Todd began.

'I am,' she said.

She turned and looked up at him, at his wide-open eyes. She wondered if this was the right time. She'd done evil. Fallen, already. What was she holding out for?

'I mixed my blood with her blood,' Frigg said, languorously. 'I mixed our blood together and then I started cursing her. I cursed all of her. I didn't want a single bit of her to escape my evil magic.

'I cursed her stubby toes, the ones she was so embarrassed about, and I cursed her slim little ankles, so delicate and breakable. I cursed her smooth legs that she never needed to shave and her knees that didn't stick out at all. I cursed her thick thighs and the boys that got between them, and I cursed her where the boys came in, and in her ass, and in her belly. I cursed her belly especially, all the parts of it. Everything inside her I listed out and I cursed. Her stomach and her spleen and her large intestine and her small one, her lungs and her liver and her heart; oh, I cursed her heart a thousand times; all of its chambers, all of its veins and arteries, and her whole nervous system. I cursed them all. I cursed her long fingers with their big fingernails, always painted bright red like her lips, which I cursed.

And I cursed her breasts that she wished were bigger, she was jealous of mine, and then her stupid white neck, almost see-through, waiting to be cut, and her face. I spent a long time cursing her face. I knew every mole of it back then. I had memorised it all. I cursed all of it. And finally, I damned her eyes, her beautiful eyes of emerald green, not dark and lonely and big and stupid like mine, and her red hair. I cursed every strand of that red hair. I cursed the way she shook it, like she knew what it was worth. Every part of her, every moment of her, every minute of her; I cursed them all.'

They were both breathing heavy now. Her skin had grown sensitive and she could feel the fear that trembled in Todd Morrow's leg. She realised he wasn't touching her. She was simply sprawled over him, like a rug over an injured man. She wanted him to touch her. She wanted him to take some active part in this thing that was happening that she didn't understand.

'And now she's dead,' she said, breathing out the words. She breathed them out into his shy, greasy little face. 'She's dead and I was the one that cursed her.

'Don't you think it's clever the way that the devil works? I asked him to curse every part of her and he did. He wrapped them all in ice. Now she's frozen there. Frozen so that I can stand over her and see every little part, every detail that I once knew so well. I see them all, held in ice, and I know that they're all just waiting. Waiting for the ice to melt, and for her whole body to fall apart.

'Oh God, I'm not even angry with her anymore,' she lifted her hand to her forehead. 'It all seems so childish. It seems so far away. A different world from a different time.'

She put her hand down, resting it on his belt as she

looked him in the eyes.

'But I did do it,' she breathed. 'I killed her. I'm a murderer.'

Then, after a pause, she whispered right into his lips.

'Can you forgive me?'

His lips trembled as hers touched them. His body was stiff. Under his mess of clothes, she felt every one of his muscles tightening. He must know, she thought, what she wanted now? She knew what she wanted. She wanted it more than anything.

'Can I?' he finally said, his lips trembling. 'Can I tell you a secret too?'

'Mmm-hmm,' she nodded. Her lips were wet, and offered to him.

'I killed her' he said.

She blinked. What was he saying? She moved closer. He was strange and delirious.

'I should tell you about it,' he said. 'I should tell you that I killed her. If I killed her then I should say. The policemen know about it, but I didn't say. You should know about it too. Before you kiss me again, you should know.'

'No,' she shook her head. 'I don't need to know. I killed her. I told you how I killed her. You don't need to have killed her as well. Just me.'

'But,' he shook his head. 'I killed her! I really did!'

She moved away.

'I don't know how.'

He was confused. Angry.

'I don't know how I did it. But I did it. I killed her. That girl. She's dead now and it was me that did it.'

Frigg stared at him. The boy's whole body was rigid. There was no way that she could get anything out of him now. Not what she wanted.

'Do you hate me?' she asked, moving away from him.

'No,' he said, shaking his head. 'No.'

'I think you hate me. For killing her.'

'I don't,' he shook his head. 'You didn't kill her. I killed her.'

She let go of his belt. The buckle was half-undone. She looked him in the eyes and saw a mix of impotence, rage and confusion. She could see all his hatred. The hatred that she used to have, directed nowhere at all, directed at all of life, undifferentiated.

'What are you?' she asked him.

In the snow-caught stone hut, Todd Morrow moaned.

Down at the river, a snowdrift fell over the body, shielding it from the world with a layer of white.

Chapter Twenty-Three

Jen Barcroft

'Let me out! You can't do this! I've not done anything wrong! Murderers! Murderers!'

'Jen,' Inspector Todor said. 'You're going to have to calm down.'

They held her in the cells for two hours. After her fit at the undertaker's she was still confused and angry.

Somehow, no one quite knew how, Jen had managed to get out onto the ice without it breaking. When the duty officer returned and found her clawing at it, thumping her fists against it, wailing and crying desperately, trying to get at her daughter, it was all she could do to call for back-up and wait. They couldn't risk another officer going under the ice.

But Jen's rage had made no difference. Tasha was still stuck under there. She was immovable. Untouchable. She had a look of blissful calm just the same, unchanging.

'I want to be under there too,' Jen thought.

But soon, tired from hammering, she'd changed her mind She stood up, stared down one last time at the body, and walked away. She walked, somehow safely, back over the ice to the riverbank.

After that, she ran. She cried. She screamed. She ended up at the undertakers. It was there that Inspector Todor picked her up.

Since then, she'd done a lot more screaming and a lot more crying. She stank of booze and cigarettes. She was emaciated, frail, with the jutting limbs that every officer recognised as a junkie. They thought she'd never shut up – not until she passed out – but after two hours she did.

Inspector Todor had questioned her immediately. As soon as she was able to speak. He had her taken to the interrogation room and had asked her a few questions. Now it looked like she was starting to rant again and he was beginning to regret his decision.

He should've left her where she was.

'Look, Jen, we want to know the answer to this as much as you do. Someone has murdered your daughter. It's a horrible crime, and nobody is judging you for getting upset. What we need from you now though, is for you to be calm. For your daughter's sake, and to help us with our investigations.'

The drink had mixed poorly with her despair. Where alcohol usually numbed her, it was now making her heart beat hard in her chest. Thump-thump thump-thump; like a freight train. Strange thoughts circled around in her mind, over and over and over.

'What have you done to her? Why can't you get her out? She's trapped!'

Todor shook his head.

'I wish we could do something, Jen. There's just not the equipment for it. The snow's covering everything. It's got worse even since you were there.'

'The snow?'

She blinked, drunk on pain that she hadn't even noticed it. She'd forgotten all about the snow, all about the ice even. She just saw her daughter, trapped. The snow burns on her knees, her nails cracked from the ice; it didn't seem real. When she thought of her daughter, trapped, she saw her trapped in plastic, trapped in glass, trapped in a horrible dream.

'The snow is severely hampering our situation,' Inspector Todor said sagely.

It was the line he was now using to the news cameras.

Jen shook silently in her chair. She didn't know where she was, but was familiar enough with the dynamic to know that this was a police interrogation.

She'd been taken in for drugs a few times in the past. A couple of drunk and disorderlies. A few illegal raves. Even a protest or two. For the other officers, a record like that meant only trouble, but the Inspector seemed different.

'I want...' Jen mumbled. 'I want... to know what happened to my daughter.'

Inspector Todor scratched at his thinning hair. He sighed and, sorry for the sufferings of the poor woman, he pulled out his chair and sat down. He looked at her across the table and leaned forward on his elbow.

'We all want to know what happened to Tasha, Jen. Trust me. I want to know as much as you.'

He sighed. He was repeating himself.

'There's a lot that we just can't tell. It makes me think back to the old days, my grandfather's time, when there was none of this DNA testing, no databases. Trying to find a killer without this stuff, it's what they used to do. It's what being a police officer was all about.

'I think we're all lost these days because the technology does so much for us, you know? I don't think of myself as a smart man, Jen, but I'm supposed to be an inspector. I'm no Sherlock Holmes. Nowadays I don't even have the concentration to read a Sherlock story all the way through. Old Conan Doyle's trying to lay out all the clues for me, and they just pass me by. When the killer's revealed, I just have to take it on Sherlock's word. I never noticed the hints along the way. I couldn't even remember them…

'That's what this case feels like to me, Jen. And I don't know why I'm telling you this, I really don't. I've not told anyone else. Your mother; she scares me. So, do the Farringdons. And the rest of them lot outside this room too. And they all have this look on their faces like they know exactly who did it, and that I'm an idiot for not working it out yet. It's like the whole world's cracked it and I'm still here, gawping around like an idiot, waiting for the big reveal.

'God…'

Todor paused in his monologue.

'It was far nicer when we could smoke in here, you know? I'm gasping.'

Jen stared at him. She'd stopped shaking along with her furious blinking. Her eyes were wide and glassy but the mania had left them.

'I'd like a smoke too,' she said.

Todor turned around, looked to the door, and then looked up at the security camera.

'Ah, bugger it,' he whispered.

He pulled out a pack of Mayfairs from his pocket and tapped the top open. Jen took one and placed it between her lips. Todor did the same.

Inspector Todor lit both cigarettes himself, knowing better than to hand her the lighter.

'Ahh, that's much better!'

Todor smiled through a cloud of smoke.

'Now, what I'm trying to say, Jen, if you'll excuse my dramatics, is that nobody here is talking to me. I'm no genius, you see. I think that's plain to all. And so, if nobody speaks to me, then there's no way that I'll work this thing out on my own. So-'

The Inspector leaned forward, moving his hand out towards Jen across the desk. Jen's hand unconsciously crept towards his. Todor noted it. She was willing to meet him half way.

'So, what I'm asking you, Jen, is if you'll speak to me? Will you tell me what you know?'

He took another drag on his cigarette and leaned forward.

'Will you help me?'

Jen's hands shook, but only lightly. No more than

normal, in fact. She lifted the cigarette to her mouth.

'Okay,' she nodded. 'What do you want to know?'

'What I want to know,' Todor said. 'Is something that I don't really know yet, if you get me? I don't know what I don't know.

'Why don't you start at the start,' he suggested. 'That's as good a place as any.'

Jen was quiet.

'Which start do you mean?'

'How about your daughter?' Todor said. 'Tell me about her. When was she born?'

'Well, I don't really know the year…'

Jen's eyes grew sad and sheepish.

'I've been in Manchester so long, you see. You lose track of time. Nobody's trying to catch you out. Nobody's forcing you to live like they do. Everyone can just be themselves, you know?'

From what Inspector Todor had gathered from Jen's records, her life in the city mostly revolved around raves and drug deals and chronic alcoholism. A   succession of partners arrested for a succession of crimes. The anonymity of the crowd has its appeal.

'So, you left Tasha with your mother, is that right?'

Jen nodded.

'I hated to do it to her. My daughter, I mean. My mum's a horrible bitch sometimes. Most of the time, actually. But she's a teacher, isn't she? She has time to look after kids. She knows how to do it.'

'She's the headteacher,' Todor agreed.

'Well there you go. She must be good at it then.'

Jen sank into herself, deflating like a slow puncture.

'I always said I'd come back when she was old enough. When Tasha could, you know, benefit from what I had to teach her and that.'

Todor made a note in his notebook, then scribbled it out.

'I know I'm not that good a role model or anything. But I think I could teach some things. Stuff that they don't teach you at school.

Jen's eyes lit up suddenly, filled with sudden panic; 'I didn't do it! I didn't kill her, you know! I might have wanted her not to be near me, but I didn't want her dead!'

'Nobody's saying that you did!' Todor said.

The moment passed. Whatever spirit it was that filled them all with guilt, it had passed straight through Jen. In and out, like a ghost through a door.

'I was going to come back one day and teach her. I really was. I just needed to get myself in a good place first. There're no good guys, you see. No offence to *you*. But guys, all of them, they're all horrible. They just take, take, take and they never give anything back. I had this guy, Danny – he was alright – but when I told him I had a kid, and that I'd just found out she was dead; guess what? He legged it. Said he couldn't handle that kind of thing. So that's another man gone. He'd seemed so nice as well...

'You see I was going to come back. I really was. I had all these plans: for Tasha, like. We could go to the salon together, get our hair done, and then go out shopping and stuff. Proper girly stuff, you know? It'd be like we were best friends; mom and daughter.'

The ash on the end of her cigarette had grown long and unstable. It hung there precariously, almost an inch in length, as she sucked vacantly on the cork and spoke about her daughter.

'I was really proud of her, you know? I heard she did really good in school. She was top of all her classes, and really popular too. Like all the popular kids, they were all looking up to her as, like, the most popular one out of all of them. And so pretty.'

Todor nodded. 'She meant a lot to you?'

'Oh yeah,' Jen said. 'Absolutely'.

The cigarette ash hovered over her knuckle, lazily fuming.

'Now,' Todor tapped his pen on his notebook. 'I don't mean to skip ahead, Jen, but this is a murder investigation and so there are certain questions that I have to ask. It's procedure, you see. I don't mean anything by it...'

Jen's eyes narrowed. The ash stood tall and trembling.

'But can I just ask,' Todor lifted his pencil. 'Where were you on the night of Tasha's murder?'

The ash slid off. It hit the table and burst with a soft poof.

'What do *you* mean by that?'

'Nothing,' Todor said. 'I just have to ask it. It's part of the procedure. I thought now was a good time.'

'Now?' Jen laughed, rage in her voice. 'What, when I'm remembering my daughter, and how much I loved her? How I was going to be a great mum and all that? Now is when you ask?'

'I wasn't implying anything by it,' Todor said.

'You were implying that I killed her!'

'No.'

'You were, *you pig*!'

Jen laughed again. It was a jagged laugh; a laugh with a single point, like a stiletto heel stamping, or a knife pushed into a chest.

Chapter Twenty-Four

Inspector Todor

'You think I killed her!'

'I don't!'

Todor shook his head. He was panicking now. What a fool he'd been. Again.

'You're a sick fucker, you know that? You and the rest of you pigs. You're all just playing mind games all the time. Trying to catch people out by seeming all nice and that, when all you really want is to throw us all in prison!'

'That's not right,' Todor said. 'No, Jen. You've got it wrong.'

'Get out!' she started screaming. 'You pig! Get out!'

The Inspector was left with a choice. Did he stay on and try to win her back, or did he leave and, in leaving, prove himself once more incapable?

There was a knock on the interrogation room door. Without thinking, Todor leapt up to answer it.

Too late he realised his decision was now made. The second he stood up, Jen began screaming. She bellowed and cried and raged furiously, at Todor and the police and the whole world all together. There'd be no getting any sense out of her now.

'What is it?' Todor snapped.

'I'm sorry to bother you, sir.'

The officer outside saluted.

'But there's a woman here. She's at front desk. She's very insistent that she see you.'

'Who is it?'

'It's a Mrs Barcroft, sir? She's the headteacher at the school-'

'Yes, I know Mrs Barcroft.'

Todor turned back to Jen. She was screaming incoherently, her finger pointed out, accusingly, but in no fixed direction.

Todor turned back to the officer.

'Go on, then. Lead on.'

They met Mrs Barcroft at reception. She was simmering in the way that only an older lady could. In her head, she was no doubt a model of comportment, and yet she gave off a furious energy, a type of wild radiation that burned the skin of anyone standing too close.

As Inspector Todor rounded the corner, he felt that mass of nuclear heat beaming directly at him.

'Inspector, let her go!'

'Now, Mrs Barcroft, this is most unusual. We are in the middle of an investigation-'

'I don't see why!'

Todor blinked. He didn't know how to respond to that.

'We know who the murderer is, Inspector! What you are doing arresting my poor suffering daughter, I don't know.'

Her voice was hard. The adjectives 'poor' and 'suffering' were delivered without a trace of empathy.

'You have arrested her, as far as I can make out, due to *pure* incompetence-'

'I have arrested her for causing affray-' Todor butted in. But she was not to be bested.

'Affray?'

'She was causing a scene at the body.'

'Grieving over her dead daughter? *My* dead granddaughter? The light of our lives? The girl who you, sir, have yet to make any progress in removing from that horrible ice?

'If it is illegal to grieve, Inspector Todor, then you best arrest me now. Arrest the rest of us while you're at it, as God knows it's only human! What the hell have you got her locked up in there for? Who do you think she's a danger to?'

'Well, to herself for one-'

'That's a monstrous assumption to make.'

Mrs Barcroft turned to the female officer.

'Only a man could make that kind of assumption. Men are as unfeeling as they are unthinking. Even this grey-jowled, hangdog example of the breed is as unfeeling as the rest of them!'

Todor extended a calming hand.

'Mrs Barcroft-'

'Don't touch me! Don't you touch me!'

Inspector Todor jumped back

Until that moment, Mrs Barcroft had been speaking quietly. Her simmering resentment came out in her words, not in her voice. The sudden burst of fury betrayed her. The sleepless nights, the long hours staring out of her office window, the tears that she shed or didn't shed and none of it seemed to make any difference to how she felt. The black beast inside her was ready to tear its way out.

'I'm sorry, Mrs Barcroft,' Todor was saying. 'But it's an ongoing investigation. You must understand.'

Mrs Barcroft swallowed, gathered herself, and then pointed her oxblood-nailed finger right into his face.

'I understand well enough, Inspector. I've written to your superiors in Manchester. They'll be hearing about all this soon enough. One of their inspectors, well aware of who the murderer is, continues to harass a bereaved family. It doesn't look good, Inspector. It doesn't look good, *at all!*'

Inspector Todor thought back to the look on William Farringdon's face. It bore a striking resemblance to Mrs Barcroft's right now. Two patriarchs, both sneering, both used to getting their way through sneering, and jabbing their fingers, and complaining to superiors. He knew that he should detest them for it, but it wasn't in his nature.

He'd only wanted a quiet life. Now, there he was, caught between two furies. Someone must be guilty. He knew that much. But he also knew that nobody would come out of this happy.

Would justice prevail? Perhaps. But even if it did, in this case, does it ever?

Inspector Todor's head grew heavy. He felt like sinking down into the floor, borne down by the weight of his pointlessness.

There is no guilty party. The guilty feel they're innocent and the innocent feel they're guilty.

'I spoke to Lucas Farringdon,' he said. 'I interrogated him for a few hours.'

Mrs Barcroft dropped her finger. She stared at him expectantly.

'Well?'

'He didn't do anything,' the Inspector said. 'I am sure of it. He has an alibi.'

'An alibi?' Mrs Barcroft's lip trembled.

'His father,' the Inspector nodded. 'His father can vouch that he was trapped inside their house when it occurred. They were snowed in.'

Mrs Barcroft shook her head. It rotated, loosely and wildly, just like her daughter's had. It was the same shaggy-dog movement. A capacity to deny everything. To shake the whole world out of their ears.

'No,' she said. 'No, it can't be.'

Inspector Todor shrugged.

'I'm afraid that it is, Mrs Barcroft.'

'No,' Mrs Barcroft repeated.

Then her head stopped shaking. She blinked hard. Her eyes searched the floor, and then the ceiling above the Inspector.

'It can't be true,' she eventually said.

She spoke calmly and quietly, her voice breathy and detached.

'It can't be true because my daughter saw him do it.'

The Inspector narrowed his eyes.

'She…'

Todor turned to the officer at his side. She looked back at him. They both stared in disbelief at Mrs Barcroft.

'She saw him do it?'

'Yes,' Mrs Barcroft nodded.

'Your daughter, Jen Barcroft, witnessed Lucas Farringdon murdering your granddaughter?'

'Yes.'

'Mrs Barcroft,' Inspector Todor said. 'You realise the seriousness of this allegation? Your daughter has been very open and honest about the fact that she didn't know about the murder until you told her, yesterday. That was the day after the body was found. Now you say that she was here all along? And, not only that, but she saw the murder herself?'

'Yes,' Mrs Barcroft said. 'And it was Lucas Farringdon who did it.'

Todor took out his notebook and wrote.

'And when did your daughter tell you this, Mrs Barcroft?'

Mrs Barcroft stood silent for a second. She stared out into the middle distance. Then, in a trance, she said; 'Yesterday. She told me yesterday.'

'But she said that *you* told *her* yesterday.'

'She's confused.' Mrs Barcroft said. 'Yes, with all the trauma. She got confused with all the trauma, and then she drank a lot as well. She's a sick girl, Inspector Todor. She gets mixed up sometimes.'

The Inspector put away his pad.

'You realise that lying to an officer of the law is an imprisonable offence, Mrs Barcroft?'

'I know,' she nodded.

Her lips grew tight, whitening with the pressure of her pursing.

'Okay,' Inspector Todor said.

He turned to the officer beside him. He gestured back to the interrogation room.

'I guess we'll go back and ask her.'

They marched back to the room. Todor strode, nervous but determined. The officer followed along behind.

Only when they opened the interrogation room door, finding Jen Barcroft in there, her face against the table, did they realise that Mrs Barcroft had been following them.

'Tell them, Jen!' she yelled through the open door. 'Tell them how you saw the Farringdon boy do it! Tell them how you saw the murder!'

Jen's head jerked up.

'Mum?'

'Goddamnit!' Todor shouted. 'Close that damn door!'

The officer pulled Mrs Barcroft back and slammed the door closed. The Inspector heard the key in the lock, followed by the muffled sound of struggle.

He turned to Jen. Jen was staring up at him, her eyes wild.

'Is it recording?' she asked, pointing to a microphone on the table.

'It's always recording,' Todor admitted. 'Even when we say it isn't.'

'He did it,' she said.

She nodded, slowly. Her eyes were wide and wild. She was grinning. Her mascara ran down her cheeks like the marks of an ancient tribe.

'The Farringdon boy did it,' she confirmed. 'I saw everything.'

'You did?'

'I did.'

Her eyes stuck out like holy beacons.

'I saw all of it. I saw him do it. He was the one. I saw all of it, and I'll testify to that.'

The Inspector looked at the microphone then down at Jen.

'So, everything you have told us up to now, about when and how you found out and about you wanting answers... all of that was a lie?'

'Yes.'

She nodded, firmly.

The Inspector took out his notebook. He held it in his hand. It was wrapped in blue leather. A gift from his last department. A parting gift. A last kiss before they betrayed him forever

He thought about it as a symbol of truth. A symbol of truth given in a spirit of falsehood. An offering made to satisfy guilt.

He couldn't bring himself to write in it. Not this. None of this.

'I see,' he said finally. 'Well, Jen, I'm sorry to say but I won't be able to let you go just yet.'

She collapsed, face-down. He looked down at her. She

seemed to have fallen immediately asleep.

Todor shook his head. What a mess.

Grimly, he lifted his walkie talkie.

'Wrigley, can we get a car out to the Farringdon's house again, please? We need to bring the boy back in. Over.'

A beep.

'Roger that, sir. We're in the neighbourhood. We'll head out there now.'

A brief pause. Another beep.

'And, sir, what shall we do about the father? If he wants to accompany the boy, sir? Over.'

The Inspector sighed and clicked the handset.

'Then let him come. In fact, bring him along. Might as well have the whole lot here. Let's get this mess sorted out, once and for all.'

Chapter Twenty-Five

—

Inspector Todor

William Farringdon slammed the patrol car door. Scout was on his wrist, barking and howling as Lucas stepped out of the car. He looked pale, his eyes sullen.

'What the hell is all this about now?' William demanded.

Inspector Todor stood on the police station steps, overcoat pulled tight around him.

'They're here, sir,' the officer at the wheel said.

He tapped his cap in a non-committal salute.

'Shall I get back to patrol?'

Todor nodded and the car's tyres span, surfing away on snow and slush.

The weather was approaching white out. That magical moment when the clouds crept in, trapping the whole world in one great snowy crystal.

The only sounds were of crunching feet and foggy breaths as they approached. Even Scout's barking, confused and unrelenting, was muffled by the air.

The Farringdons had spent every moment since Lucas' arrest in a state of not-yetness. They knew they should move on. They knew that sitting and thinking, letting the horrible details of the case, the knowns and the terrifying unknowns, wash over them, would soon drive them to despair. They knew they must carry on. But they couldn't. Not yet.

And so up at the Farringdon household the man and boy sat in different rooms. Objects of interest in front of them but their minds were elsewhere. Scout went unwalked.

They were frozen, like Helen Farringdon up in her drunken bed. Waiting for enough time to pass, to feel right again, unsure if such a time would ever come.

'Look at the boy!' William shouted at the Inspector. 'Have you not done enough? His childhood sweetheart dead. His reputation in tatters. Is it not enough?'

'I'm sorry. I wasn't left with any other option.'

William's moustache twitched.

'What do you mean by *that*?'

William stood tall, proud and imposing; over-compensating. Lucas was tired, loose, hunched; almost crushed. Inspector Todor recognized the faces of the wrongly accused.

And yet, in his sad life, Todor had sometimes seen those same innocent faces worn by the guilty. By people whose guilt was beyond doubt.

The duplicity of men tired him. His own incapacity to fathom it was humiliating. He was so far away from the killer…

'Just come in,' he motioned to the two men and their dog. 'You'll find out inside.'

Their wellies squeaked on the doormat.

'There he is! It's him!'

Mrs Barcroft started shouting the second she saw them enter. She dashed forward with a painted nail outstretched, reaching as if to pop the boy's head like a balloon.

'Hey!' William Farringdon pushed his son behind him. 'What's all this then? What's going on, eh?'

Scout barked harder, growling at the teacher.

'Keep that beast away from me!' Mrs Barcroft yelled, pointing her talon at the springer spaniel.

Inspector Todor shoved in through the door behind them. Mrs Barcroft had pushed the men backwards, blocking their entry.

'Officers!' Todor cried out. 'Is there anyone here? We're in need of assistance!'

Mrs Barcroft and William were yelling, Scout was barking, and no one anywhere seemed to be listening. Or, if they were, they didn't seem to care.

'I should have known it was you!'

Mrs Barcroft pointed her finger now, finally and inevitably, at William Farringdon.

'Thinking you can come into a small town like ours and live off everyone's goodwill. You should have stayed in the city! You should have stayed there with the other snobs and the other rich layabouts that can't control their children!'

'You're barking mad, woman!' he yelled back, moustache ruffling with each indignant snort.

'Your damn daughter was a tear away and your granddaughter no better! I have no idea what horrible mess she got herself into, but it was nothing to do with my boy! We've done nothing wrong. It's you Barcrofts. You mess with trouble, you get trouble!'

'Us, trouble?! That's rich coming from a house of alcoholic booze hounds!'

Mrs Barcroft's face grew red and purple, the bluster swelled in her features like a tropical storm.

'You're a lot of stinking drunks! Your son's a bad influence. Your wife and daughter are basket cases. Everyone knows to avoid you in this town and *everyone knows he killed her!*'

'What!?'

William bellowed. The edges of his mouth cracked with the strain.

'You would accuse him? Despite no evidence? Based only on your own ugly thoughts in your own ugly, dried up and delusional mind? You're a monster! You're a beast, woman!'

Todor watched, helpless to intervene.

It was vaudeville, really. He would laugh if it weren't so bleak.

The Inspector turned to Lucas. The boy was cowering behind his father.

'Come, lad.' Todor grabbed the boy's arm. 'Come with me, why don't you?'

Mrs Barcroft and William Farringdon were yelling over each other now. Jabbing fingers at each other's chests, then pointing off to the horizon; sometimes in the direction of the murder scene, sometimes in the direction of the prison cells. They weren't even responding to each other anymore, simply hurling their accusations into each other's faces.

Seeing his son walking away with the Inspector, William shouted.

'Where are you taking him?!'

'I'm just taking the boy to get some water. There are no formal charges here. If you'll just remain calm, sir-'

'There *should* be charges!' Mrs Barcroft yelled. 'He did it! He murdered her! We all know it! You should have him in cuffs already!'

'You psychopathic bitch!' William snarled.

As the fight between the patriarch and the matriarch continued, Inspector Todor led Lucas away.

The Inspector took him down a corridor, through a pair of swing doors. Suddenly the station was quiet again. After the intensity of the shouting match, the quiet now seemed mystical, as if they'd stepped through a magic portal.

Todor remembered the waiting room. It was barely used now. Most prisoners simply walked out, or else met their loved ones at the front door. The room was always empty. Todor held open the door and guided Lucas in.

They looked around at the sparse and sanitary room. Four chairs, lined with plastic, a coffee table with a stack of magazines, decades old, and a floor which had been cleaned more times than it had been walked on.

'Where are we?' Lucas asked.

'It's a quiet place.'

Todor guided him to a seat.

'Why don't you take a seat and get comfortable? We might be here a while.'

Lucas flushed white.

'I…' he stuttered. 'I-'

'It's okay. It's okay.'

The Inspector patted the boy's shoulder.

Lucas sat, shivering. He lifted his legs up into his body and rubbed his shins. It wasn't cold, at least, not in there. The snow was falling heavy outside but the waiting room had no windows; only a clock and bare, blue-tinted walls. The rest of the world seemed far away.

'Now,' Todor said. 'I'm going to leave you here for a moment, Lucas. Your dad and the headteacher are kicking up quite the fuss outside. I best go see to that before we sit down for our chat, okay?'

Lucas nodded.

Then, just as the Inspector twisted the door handle and made to leave, Lucas spoke.

'I might have done it,' he choked. 'I might have.'

Todor turned.

'What's that, Lucas?'

'Maybe I did kill her?'

He sniffed, voice wobbling. If he kept talking his sniff would turn to tears and he'd be left crying again over his guilt.

Maybe that's what I deserve, his eyes seemed to say. *Maybe I ought to be guilty.*

'What do you mean that you *might* have killed her?' Todor asked.

'I mean,' Lucas sobbed. 'I don't know what I mean. Maybe I did? Maybe it was me.

'Everyone thinks it's me,' he said. 'Everyone looks at me like I did it. I don't think I did it but maybe I did? Maybe it was me who caused it, by saying or doing something?'

Suddenly, he started slapping at his head.

'I'm so stupid sometimes! I'm so uncaring! Unthoughtful! I hurt everyone. Everyone! I'm hurting everyone all the time and I don't know how to stop it because I don't even know I'm doing it!'

Inspector Todor walked up to the boy and grabbed his hand.

'But you were with your father, weren't you? On the night it happened? And for two weeks before that? You were snowed in?'

Tears leaked from Lucas' eyes.

'I don't know,' he shrieked. 'I don't remember anything now! I think I was but maybe I wasn't? Maybe I was dreaming? Maybe I didn't kill her, but I made her kill herself?'

'What? You're not making sense, Lucas.'

'I must have hurt her somehow!' he yelled. 'Don't you get it? I must've somehow done something and caused her to die! God, I'm such a stupid, stupid idiot!'

Todor grabbed both of Lucas' wrists, stopping him before he could pummel himself any further.

The boy's teeth were chattering now hysterically, overcome by memories, flooding in from times long past.

Chapter Twenty-Six

Lucas Farringdon

It was his birthday. Maybe one or two - perhaps all of his birthdays together? No. No, it was the birthday after his sister had left. He loved Jo, but she was gone. He was going to have a good birthday, even without her. He knew it.

His friends. He invited the whole class around. They were ten, twelve, thirteen years old? Old enough to be there alone. It was just him, his friends, and his mum. Where was his dad? He couldn't remember. Maybe he wasn't there at all?

All he remembered of that moment. The moment when they'd brought out the cake and everyone sang happy birthday. He'd closed his eyes to make a wish. What had he wished for? He couldn't remember. Something silly. A new bike or a video game. Maybe even for his sister to come back.

He blew out his candles, and then his mother began. *'It looks like you got your wish already,'* she said. Something along those lines. The words themselves he couldn't remember, only the pain of hearing them. *'You got what you wished for,'* she said. *'You chased her away.*

I don't know what you did, but you went and did it. You made her leave. You made it so she won't come back, not ever again. You made it so she won't even call us.'

'You're a horrible, selfish little boy. Do you want to have your birthday present? I bet you do. You just take, take, take, don't you? Well, guess what, your father's taken it. It was in his car when he left. He's gone now. So, I guess you won't be having it, and it'll serve you right for driving your sister away from us.'

He remembered it all now, flooding back like a horrible dream. His mother there, wine glass in her thin hand, the sneer on her face that came out late in the drunken night. It'd been out then too, early, in the mid-morning. He couldn't remember the time exactly. All his friends had looked on, watching her as she snarled at him. They watched him as he sat, dumbfounded, open-mouthed, and confused.

Maybe he'd done something? What, he couldn't remember.

All his life he'd thought about it. Maybe he'd done something? His father had told him not to worry. Even if he'd done something, nobody cared, nobody remembered. He'd buried the thought deep down. Laying it beneath the foundations of his happy life, buried down there like a body.

But perhaps he'd done something? Perhaps he'd done it then? Perhaps he'd done it again? He wasn't like the rest. He was solely, personally, and completely responsible.

Chapter Twenty-Seven

Inspector Todor

'I don't know why,' Lucas shook and sobbed. 'But I killed her. I killed her. I really did. It was me. It was all me.'

Inspector Todor shook his head.

Whatever it was that was in the air that winter, it was catching. He was sure of it.

Todor wondered then if it was his own wishful thinking or his own guilty desires – longing for a perp, any perp – that had brought all of this mess about. In his longing for a guilty party, he'd conjured guilt in the heart of everyone. Even, perhaps, himself come to think of it. Perhaps now it was his fault, too?

'No,' he said, patting Lucas on the shoulder. 'I don't think it was you, boy. Don't worry your confused   little head about it.'

Lucas looked up at him, face red, and sniffing.

'You get your breath back, son. It's not your fault. Not any of this. I'm going to see to it that we get this thing resolved, somehow or another. You sit here and I'll be back soon.'

Lucas nodded, the tears having stopped.

'Would you like a cup of tea, son?'

'Yes, please,' he whispered.

'Alright,' Todor smiled. 'I'll have the shift officer bring you one. Now, if only I could bloody find her, eh?'

Lucas smiled, weakly. Todor winked and strode down the corridor, back in the direction of the entrance hall.

As he approached he could hear the shouting and barking grow louder. The parents were laying into each other, their voices hoarse.

Todor paused.

He stood there for a second, listening and thinking. Then, with an awkward click of his heels, he span round and walked back on himself, heading straight to the interrogation room, where he'd left Jen.

As the Inspector opened the door, Jen lifted her head. By the look of the tabletop, she'd been asleep when he entered. She rubbed away the drool with a sleeve.

Chapter Twenty-Eight

Jen Barcroft

The short nap had sobered her up a little. Her daughter's death was still there, ringing in her ears, but the world was calmer now. She felt like a ship that had escaped a heavy storm. She was lost at sea, yes, but at least the raging winds had calmed down and the sun, with all its pathos, was shining warm.

'Inspector,' she said, voice husky.

He nodded and she looked at him, eyes watery.

'Where's my mum? Was she here?'

The Inspector nodded.

'Your mum's here, Jen. She's come to collect you. We're letting you go. That whole business on the ice was dangerous, yes, but understandable given the circumstances.'

Her lip trembled.

'And my daughter?'

'We're busy tracing the killer now,' he nodded. 'Don't you worry about that. We'll have them in no time at all. We thank you for all the information you gave us. You were very helpful.'

'But, I-'

A fuzziness filled her head as she thought about the interview. She couldn't remember much now. Not the words, just the strange and terrible feeling of guilt.

'I'm not sure if what I told you was right,' she said, shaking loose the cobwebs. 'I don't know if I said the right thing.'

Todor held the door for her.

'You did well, Jen. As good as anyone could've done, given the circumstances. You get your things together now and we'll get ready to sign you out.'

He lifted his walkie talkie and double-tapped the button.

'Yes, Inspector?' came the voice of the duty sergeant.

'Can we prepare the younger Ms Barcroft for signing out, please, sergeant? She'll need collecting from the interrogation room. Give her back her things, and then if you could take her to the waiting room before she goes, I'd be much obliged. Over.'

'Roger that, sir. Over.'

Jen looked up at him.

'So, I'm free to go?'

'Of course!'

Jen stood, swaying for a moment with shock, leaning her full body weight on the table.

'You know, Inspector,' she said. 'I don't know why, but I felt a terrible weight over me just then. Like I was never going to leave here. Like, finally, after all these years, something had caught up with me that really ought to have killed me a long time ago.

'It's hard to explain,' she said. 'But it felt right. That I was going down, you know. Prison. It felt right. But now, now that I think about it clearly, I; I really can't think of anything I've done that would lead to it.'

Inspector Todor nodded.

'Well, you just wait here, Jen. Gather your thoughts. You'll be out soon. The duty sergeant will be down to collect you in a moment and she'll take care of you. You'll be out of here soon.'

Chapter Twenty-Nine

Jen Barcroft

Jen looked down at the table, acquiescing. Todor gazed at her for a moment, then returned to the fight at reception.

'It's no wonder your wife drinks!' Mrs Barcroft was yelling. 'With an oaf of a man like you around! You drove her to it, no doubt. And your daughter too! She was a good girl at school. When she could get away from *your* horrible house. She was an ideal student! Your toxic family and you, you horrible man, you soured her and now she's run away – and it's a good thing too!'

'You would talk about my family, you dried up old coot? As if the Farringdons are anywhere near the low and slimy level of the Barcrofts! Single mothers! Drunkards! Maniacs! Your daughter's a drunken maniac. You're a religious mad puritan! It doesn't take much imagination to know which way your granddaughter was going to go! I told Lucas, I told him – stay away from that girl. She's nice enough but she's from a family of maniacs!'

'How dare you talk about my granddaughter, you murderer! A family of murderers! Liars! Cheaters! You had your rabid boy drown her and now you're covering up for him!'

'Religious maniac! Puritan! Go and burn some other witches and leave us alone!'

'If you'll excuse me-' Inspector Todor said.

The two stopped yelling and Scout stopped barking. They all looked at the Inspector.

'I'm terribly sorry for wasting both of your times,' he said, with a mock gravity. 'It was all in the service of our investigations and, I'm pleased to say, I can now roundly conclude that this particular stage of the investigation is complete.'

'Yes?' Mr Farringdon said, snorting.

Mrs Barcroft raised an eyebrow.

'And you found him guilty, yes? The boy?'

William grimaced beneath his moustache.

'We shall be letting both of your children go,' Inspector Todor announced. 'Now, if you'll follow me, you will find them in the waiting room.'

The parents' anger bubbled behind him as he led them down the corridor. Their feet tapped on the tiled floors, while Scout padded softly behind, pulled along behind on her lead. She sniffed the ground, wagging her tail.

Todor was proud of himself then. He just had to hope it would work. If it had done, then he'd finally have pulled off something worthy of an Inspector, no longer a nothing and a nobody.

Yes, he saw. Yes, it had worked.

The two suspects, Jen and Lucas, sat in the waiting room together. Neither recognising the other, politely waiting to be excused. Neither knew that the other was in there with regards to Tasha's murder.

'Farringdons, Barcrofts,' Todor span on his heel and announced. 'You are both free to go.'

'But what about-' Mrs Barcroft began.

'Mrs Barcroft, I will on this occasion ignore the deception that both you and your daughter sought to thrust upon Her Majesty's Police. As you can see, your daughter, who you said was a witness to the entire murder, has been sat for the past five minutes alongside the boy that she supposedly saw doing the killing.'

'You're Lucas Farringdon?' Jen asked.

Lucas nodded, sheepishly.

'And Mr Farringdon,' the Inspector continued. 'You need to consider your tone when conversing with police inspectors. If it wasn't for your boy's total sincerity then I would've taken you for the murderers. It was only after speaking to the lad that I realised what I didn't understand about you, and which's that you were trying to cover up a crime that never existed.'

'Cover up?'

William huffed, face reddening.

'I've never heard of anything so preposterous in all my life!'

The Inspector thanked the sergeant on duty, who appeared at that moment with Jen's personal effects. He was glad that another member of the police was present to witness his small but cunning victory.

'Now, I don't know what dark pasts you have in your family histories, and, frankly, I don't really want to know. We all have things in our pasts we're not proud of. The fact is, you've turned this murder inquiry into some kind of interfamilial spat and I'm tired of it.

'There *is* a murderer,' he nodded. 'Somewhere out there. On the loose. I'm tired of being called away from the search because you lot can't see past your mutual recriminations. I know it's not my place to say, but where I come from a bit of forgive and forget would be what's called for here.

'But I know you English are stubborn people, so I'll be content if you all just got out of my station for now, please. We have important matters to deal with. It's time for you to go home and grieve, and leave the business of working this out to us, the professionals.'

Slowly, silently, the two broken families gathered their things and huddled out of the station. Inspector Todor reflected how, in the right circumstances, the two families were quite a match for each other.

One big gang of misery, they could've been,   projecting their own failings out on everyone else.

Two police cars had pulled up, waiting to take the families home.

William held open the door for Lucas. The boy looked shaken but less pale. Perhaps he was finally relieved.

Jen held the door open for her mother. Mrs Barcroft was the one shaking now; her daughter was stable, almost sober.

Inspector Todor looked to the duty sergeant, a victorious grin creeping along his face. He had a twinkle in his eye. Finally, a turn of good luck. He was almost getting the hang of it.

'Inspector,' the duty sergeant said, her face grave. 'We've received an emergency call. It's from the forest, near the body. A girl's being attacked. She says it's the murderer.'

'Oh my God!' the Inspector cried. 'Where are the officers? The ones that should be down there watching the body? Are they in radio contact?'

As he reached down to his walkie talkie, the duty sergeant coughed. He looked up.

All of his triumph dropped out of him like stones through a paper bag.

'The two cars you just withdrew, sir, to take the Farringdons and the Barcrofts home; those were the ones guarding the crime scene.'

The Inspector swore.

The humiliation alone, he hoped, might just kill him.

'What do you want us to do, Inspector?' the duty sergeant asked. 'The call's ended. The girl's in trouble.'

'Shit,' the Inspector replied. 'Shit!'

He looked up at her. She didn't flinch. Angry, maybe or just disappointed? Perhaps she just saw him how he truly was: a worm.

'You stay here,' he said to her. 'My car's parked around back. I'll go. Once our guests have been delivered home safely, you send those cars over to me. I might need back up.'

'You're going down there yourself?'

'Yes.'

'Unarmed? No back-up?'

'I told you!' he whined. 'You should send me back-up as soon as those cars get the families home. I've caused this damn mess and it's only fitting I be the one to sort it all out, you see? And, with all this snow, there'll be no bloody radio contact down there anyway.'

'It's set to get worse,' the duty sergeant said. 'The snow.'

'I know.'

The snow grew deeper, inch upon inch, piling up every moment. it was falling heavy, clumps the size and shape of hands upturned to God.

'Send the back-up,' Inspector Todor said. 'Just send the damn back-up. I'll be back here with the killer soon. Get one of the cells ready.'

The duty sergeant nodded and went back inside.

Chapter Thirty

Frigg McBride

The sound inside Todd Morrow's hut was softly dampened, like a pillow had been pressed over it. The fire crackled weakly and the thick layer of snow outside shielded the two cold inhabitants from the wind.

'Please, don't-' Todd said as Frigg moved closer.

The warmth of the fire and the red light catching on the woodsman's tools. The scent from dried skins and hanging herbs, all made Frigg think of a time without time. They were locked, her and the strange boy, in the dark primordia of the world.

'It's just us two out here,' she said. 'Nobody else. Just us.'

He was breathing heavily, she noticed.

'Are you okay?' she asked. 'Did I do something? What did I say?'

'I did it!' He sobbed. 'Why don't you say anything? I did it!'

'Did what?'

'I killed her! I'm the killer! I killed the girl that bullied you.'

Frigg frowned at him, impatient.

'I know, and I said that I killed her too. We all did. Is

that really what's getting to you?'

'But you're not *listening*!'

He threw his arms up.

'You're not listening to me. You didn't do it – I did! I'm the killer, not you!'

'You?' she asked. 'But… what do you mean?'

'I mean it was *me*, okay?'

He started shaking his hands in front of his mouth, trying to tear words out. Words that would finally say what he wanted to say.

'You?' Frigg mumbled. 'You…'

'I did it!' he yelled.

Then, in one huge roll, like an elephant lying down to die, Todd Morrow collapsed back into his chair. Frigg stood, looking down on him as he heaved there, heaped in his winter's skin.

'I'm-' she started.

'Are you going to leave me?' he asked, pathetically.

'No,' she said. 'No, I'm not leaving you.'

'Are you going to tell everyone?' he sniffed.

'No,' she shook her head. 'No, it's just a lot of information. I'm… I'm going to go and get some air.'

'You're going to leave me…'

'No,' she said. 'No, no. Nothing like that. Just air. I'm just going for air.'

When she went to the door she found it frozen shut. The thought of it – being trapped – sent a wave of panic rushing through her body. She chuckled nervously, then threw all her force against the door. It gave a little.

'Just a bit of air,' she said, watching his heaped body.

He was turned away from her.

She threw all her weight into it, slamming her shoulder into the door. With relief, she felt it give. With another push, the hut's door swung open, releasing her into the forest.

The snow was falling. It was always falling. She'd forgotten how they'd arrived at Todd's dwelling. Despite coming there twice now, she'd no memory of the route. The clouds were sinking down now too, and the narrow valley threatened a whiteout.

She closed the door softly behind her. Part of her wanted to slam it and lean some big rock against it. But she would never manage it. She also knew Todd Morrow was a strange boy and that, for all his emotional outbursts, he could still be making it all up. He seemed the type who would let his own stories carry him away. He believed his own words too quickly, what few of them he had.

Perhaps, she thought, he was the killer? But he didn't seem the type.

As she took a few steps and looked back at the hut, crouching there in the snow, she then thought perhaps he was. Perhaps he had killed Tasha. And maybe he'd even kill again.

She took a few steps more.

She kept walking and with each step the thought followed her. The ground beneath her feet was slippery, branches, leaves, and mossy stones all buried beneath three or four inches of snow. She recalled how hard it had been to get up there when the snow was thin. Now she could see nothing, and the afternoon sun was low and waning, flattening the ground. She stumbled more than once as she waded out into the snow.

Frigg didn't know where she was going, or what she was going to do. She hoped she'd look down the valley and see a way out but, as she pushed past a holly bush, she realised the lower valley was now all lost to the whiteout.

Up above, she could no longer see the treetops, where only the lower branches were visible. Stranded in a thin band of fogless winter and lost in the white.

There was an incline on her left which rose slightly before dropping down into a bowl. Everything she said and did up there could be heard from the hut. If she spoke, whispered even, it would get blown back to Todd where he lay in his warm and sorrowful heap.

She climbed down into the bowl, hoping that, from there at least, she could speak without him hearing.

She looked down at her hand which gripped her phone. She'd already dialled 999, looking in the direction of the hut. No, he shouldn't be able to hear. The phone was already at her ear.

'Police,' she heard herself say.

The operator was talking. All she could think of was Todd Morrow as if he were on the call as well and that he could hear every word spoken down the line.

She turned from the hut. *Point your voice away*, she told herself. *Point it away so he can't hear.*

'I'm somewhere,' she said, sniffling now. 'Somewhere near the crime scene, where Tasha Barcroft was murdered.

The man I'm with, he says he's the murderer. He says he killed her. I'm really scared. Can you send someone please?'

The voice spoke but she couldn't hear it. Something about officers at the crime scene, but they had just been withdrawn.

'Please,' she said. 'Just hurry.'

She hung up. It was all she could take as the panic was in her now. She didn't know what to do. She *couldn't* go back, but she'd *have* to go back.

She turned and he was there.

Todd Morrow stood at the lip of the bowl looking down on her, grief in his eyes. She shuddered and every muscle in her body rippled.

'Did you-?' she began.

He nodded. He'd heard everything or enough to know, at least.

Panic ran red through her veins as he took a step forward. She turned and ran, hearing him follow.

She ran without screaming. Ran, breath wild, arms tearing on bushes and branches, sleeves left in pieces along the way. Behind her, she could hear his animal grunting, his cries; half-threat, half-moan.

She ran blindly into the white fog which sunk low. She pushed blindly through, the wind lashing, snow crashing into her, lunging into hail like fists. The ice hit her face and legs. He was behind her. Close, then further away, then horribly close.

She reached the bottom of a dip and then began to climb. It was there that he had her. She heard breathing, a gruff and wordless yell. She felt a hand on her leg and fell.

Frigg turned over in the snow and saw the madness of his eyes. Todd Morrow was lost to her now. The beast was loose inside him. He clattered his teeth together, eyes wide and staring. The horrible look of an innocent trapped in a raging body. A mad animal.

He had her leg and crawled up at her. Todd had fallen too, just as Frigg fallen. She knew he'd soon be on top of her. She lifted a leg and smashed her boot as hard as possible into his face.

He reeled back, grabbing for his nose, gushing blood. She kicked at him again, losing her boot in the process.

Frigg jumped up and ran. She ran and ran, caring nothing for where she went. All she wanted was to be away. All directions, right now, led away. The breath heaved hot in her chest and her cheeks stung with the cold, but she ran and nothing else.

Soon she couldn't hear him anymore.

She stopped, gasping, her heart ready to explode. She leaned against a tree and looked around. He wasn't behind her, didn't seem to be anywhere. She, too, was lost.

She was lost in the middle of a frozen forest in full whiteout. Every slippery rock and piece of jagged wood was hidden beneath a layer of snow. The cold was moving quickly in on her and so, she reminded herself, was Todd Morrow, the killer, the wild man of the woods.

She limped on with no way back. Only forwards. If only she knew where that lead.

Chapter Thirty-One

Inspector Todor

Todor pulled up at the edge of the forest, checking his mobile. No signal. A couple of clicks on the walkie talkie showed the same. All signals were down.

He sat in the car for a moment, watching as tufts of snow slid into focus. Patches of white falling from white air. He thought about the murderer, down there, waiting for him. A killer unidentified but, by now, perhaps already drenched in the blood of a second victim. Todor's heart thumped in his chest.

Then he thought of his own humiliations. The endless stream of them that all seemed to culminate in this very spot. The ginnel between the houses. The path down to the crime scene. As soon as he'd landed in this town, this crime had been waiting for him. It'd been lurking there, preparing itself for his arrival.

It had humiliated him. Now, he sighed, supposing it would end him altogether… perhaps such no bad thing.

Then lastly, he thought of the girl. She was being chased around down there by a monster. If Todor died, at least it would be in rescuing her. A hero's end, maybe.

He blinked an image of a flower-strewn hearse out of his mind and opened the door.

The car was already covered in snow an inch thick. It was coming down fast. He lifted his hat from the dashboard and screwed it on his head.

He blew warm air on his hands, rubbing them together. Then entered the forest.

Chapter Thirty-Two

Frigg McBride

Frigg was lost. She'd known that for minutes now; long, long minutes. Her heart beat fast then slow, fast then slow, as the full weight of her situation hit her. It receded, giving way to a tactical mind, a spirit of survival, only then to come back, hitting her again with a wave of terror and hopelessness.

She saw a black tree rising from fog. Had she doubled back? The horrible thought struck her that perhaps she was back at Todd's hut. Had she come in a circle?

With the white so close in it was hard to tell whether the land sloped up or down.

Her feet plunged through the snow. One, then the next. One, then the next. Crunching and squeaking.

The ground beneath was strewn with leafy debris. Slime beneath the crust. Each step threatened to trip her, send her sprawling down the hill. Perhaps she'd fall on a spike and impale herself or crack her skull open on a mossy rock.

Then, she heard something. Another creaking. Another scratching sound of something moving out there that wasn't her. Something, or someone.

As Frigg stepped past the tree, she found she was standing on the verge of a steep slope. One more step and she'd have plummeted down, rolling into the white abyss. There was no way to tell where the bottom was.

The sound approached her. Whichever way she turned it seemed to be behind her. She tried to quiet her heavy breathing, but could hear nothing but her own lungs.

She span around and around, dizzying herself. She couldn't remember where the drop was.

Then, a burst of movement!

She threw herself back, away from the sound.

She fell, down and down. There was nothing where the floor should be. Instead, she fell through the air for what felt like minutes. Down, down, down; into the drop.

As she fell, her brain finally registered the movement. It had been a squirrel. Only a squirrel which had run down the tree trunk beside her.

Too late now to see that. She hit the slope, landing square on her back. The air slapped out of her. Frigg lay for a second, unable to breathe, and then started to tumble.

She rolled down the slope on and on. In the white out all she could see was the bouncing of her own limbs as she bumped off rocks and branches. The remains of brambles tore at her legs and arms. Her face was sliced by a loose, jagged bit of wire; perhaps from some ancient fallen fence. She seemed to slide forever.

Eventually, she hit the floor as the slope levelled off and was left lying on frozen rocks. The last rocks of the valley had smashed into her, bruising her along her legs and back.

Winded, broken, bleeding, Frigg blinked, rubbed her eyes, and tried to look around.

She was at the crime scene.

The scene was still.

Down there at the bottom of the valley, the snow seemed to have eased a little. She looked up and saw the tight basket of branches that caught most of the snowfall. The trees held it aloft like a dark blanket overhead.

The fog had receded here too, she realised. If she could see the treetops, perhaps she had a chance of seeing her pursuer.

She tried lifting her head but couldn't, still too rattled from the fall. Her breath was slowly seeping back into her, but she wasn't breathing easy just yet.

As Frigg lay on the ground, her ears to the freezing rock, she heard the minute cracking of ice. Echoing from somewhere, she heard the trickle of the river. The river was moving again, she thought happily. Life was returning, deep beneath the ice.

When she finally pulled herself up, she saw nothing of Todd Morrow. She dared to hope he was lost, fallen somewhere in his own forest and now stranded. She even hoped he'd given up and back to his shack. Perhaps, she told herself. But still her eyes darted every which way, his silhouette lingering at the corner of her eye.

Frigg dragged herself over to the side of the frozen pool. Tasha Barcroft was still out there. The girl beneath the ice.

Frigg wanted to see her again. In death that horrible girl who was so beautiful.

She limped to the bridge and, leaning on the   creaking

stone, she carried her slippery feet up its arc. Her one shoeless sock was sodden.

She looked down from the middle of the bridge. Tasha was almost invisible below a thick layer of powder which obscured the ice, her face totally covered by snow. All Frigg could see of her were outstretched hands and a hint of red hair, curling around in the frozen water.

Frigg sat there, leaning out. She felt her bruised breath leaving her chest, warm, only to freeze on the air.

Then, she heard a second pair of lungs behind her.

She turned, and saw that it was Todd Morrow.

Where had he been? Hanging from the side of the bridge? Waiting down on the ice? Lying in wait behind the trees?

Before she could scream, he jammed a hand into her mouth. She fought and bit and tried to get away but he pushed her hard against the side of the bridge. A stone gave way with the impact, falling down and smashing onto the ice below. The two of them lost their footing and fell, tearing at each other on the icy stone.

'It's all a mistake!' Todd Morrow screamed at her. 'A mistake!'

His bellowed, raw and barking like a wolf. The howl of a predator. She kicked at him and flung her fists.

'A mistake!' he yelled once more, only to choke as her knee struck his groin.

He doubled up. She wrestled with her feet, forced them to stand up. Shuddering, she tried to make them run. She made it a few steps off the bridge before Todd leapt.

His terrible leap landed him square behind her, arm

around her ankle. Frigg turned but tripped and fell, leg wrenching from its socket.

The side of the bridge gave way and the two of them rolled down, onto the ice. A hail of loose stones smashed around them. The sides of the bridge plunged into the river, punching holes through the ice.

Frigg broke away from Todd and made to run. But she couldn't. Her leg was out of its socket. She couldn't move. Couldn't stand.

She felt herself tip over and the river rose to meet her. Frigg clattered face-first onto the sheet ice and skidded out, sprawling along its surface.

Todd, was, somehow, on his feet. Standing there, his baggy assemblage of clothes hanging from him like rags from a skeleton. His frail body was moved by an uncertain power. Eyes hollow and undarting. He moved as in a dream.

'Stop!' a voice called out.

Frigg and Todd stopped.

They looked out into the whiteout, seeing a figure approach. The voice was Welsh, ringing like music.

Chapter Thirty-Three

Inspector Todor

'Don't move you two! The ice!' it called. 'It's breaking up all around you!'

Inspector Todor had battled his way down the arching path. He'd been expecting to have a fruitless search through the snow, or perhaps a life-or-death brawl, but instead found these two. Children really. They were leaping about like they were playing some kind of game.

A deadly game, out there on the ice.

Huge fractures were appearing in the ice. From where Todor stood, the break-up was obvious. Huge snaps and booms accompanied the bursting ice. Each crack sent fountains of frozen mist shooting up into the air. The two figures staggered around with no sense of the danger all around them.

Todd looked at the Inspector. The hat gave him away as police. The same police who had taken him away that first time, in fact. The policeman was staggering down the slope towards him. Todd looked down at the girl.

He leapt at her.

Frigg was prepared. She saw the bend in his legs knew

his intention. As Todd leapt in a clear, rounded arc, up and over, aiming to come down right on top of her, she rolled towards and under him. Todor watched him fly above her before Morrow's face hit the ice.

Frigg found herself staring straight down into the eyes of the girl beneath the ice. She lay on top of her. Up close, the majesty of her eyes was even more beautiful.

Todd turned, nose and lips bleeding. The warm blood ran free of his face and down onto the ice where his huge leap had cracked it.

Morrow cowered there, looking once at Frigg and then once at the Inspector. Then, with a sound like the cracking of a whip, the ice gave way beneath him.

Todd Morrow didn't have time to scream. He plunged down into freezing cold water and beneath the ice. The power of the stream, compressed underneath the weight of frozen water, sucked him far below. He was dragged, kicking, panicking, blowing huge bubbles, yards and yards beneath the piled-up ice.

On the surface, all they could hear was the sound of his hammering hands. Hammering and thrashing against the impossible weight above him. The knocking moved downstream, away from the hole he'd made.

Then, eventually, there was no knocking left at all.

Wherever Todd was when he died didn't matter. His body would continue on; pushed downriver by the thaw. One of the many people who had admitted to the killing of Tasha Barcroft was now dead. *Let us hope*, the Inspector thought, *that this was the right one.*

'Help!' Frigg cried out.

Too late, the Inspector realised that, as he'd sat listening to the struggles of Todd Morrow, the girl remained out there, still in danger. The ice was breaking all around her.

'Stay calm!' he shouted. 'I'm coming down there. We'll figure something out. Just don't move! It's crucial that you don't move!'

Frigg nodded. She was lying right on top of Tasha. Tasha, trapped there, the girl beneath the ice, seemed to be giving some stability to the ice all around her. As the rest of the river broke up into smaller and smaller chunks, the ice around Tasha held firm.

Frigg clung to the top of it. She felt it move.

The river was turning to slush around her. It was moving again. Bursting, it seemed, free from its long slumbers. Frigg felt herself carried along. The block of ice bobbed, loose, and moving slowly downstream. Tasha's blissful eyes stared up at Frigg. The ecstatic half-smile on her lips seemed to be watching over her now, telling her that everything would be okay.

'Here!' the Inspector called.

He'd managed to reach the bridge. There was almost nothing of it left now. Both sides had fallen down into the water and all that still stood was an arc of slippery stone.

Inspector Todor didn't think twice. He launched himself onto the arc. He scrambled up the stonework. His legs kicked away beneath him, feeling the ice beneath and the cold rearing up like flames. If he fell, it was all over.

'Here!' he shouted again. 'Take my hand!'

Frigg swallowed. The ice floe was pushing her towards the bridge. She reached up but, there, almost catching it – her fingers slipped.

She felt a moment of certain doom. Her one chance of escape lost. The ice would melt away and she would die an agonising death, freezing solid in the water.

'Don't worry!'

Inspector Todor breathed heavily, spinning himself around.

'We have a second chance!'

Passing under the bridge, the world went dark. Then, just in front of her, Frigg saw the silhouette of a hand reaching down. The Inspector was leaning right out over the side of the bridge. One wrong move and he'd fall in himself. But he was risking it all. He was willing to risk his life if it meant giving Frigg a second chance at hers.

'I can see it!'

Frigg cried out. Tears falling freely down her cheeks.

'I've got it!'

And their two hands met.

Pivoting himself awkwardly, Inspector Todor heaved the young girl up from the ice. Frigg clambered up over him and onto the cold wet stone of the bridge.

'Come on!' she called to the Inspector. 'There's no time.'

Sure enough, as they crawled away from the bridge, desperate and exhausted, the last stones of that old grey arc gave way and, with a terrible plunging splash, it collapsed into the water.

'We need back up,' the Inspector was saying into his walkie-talkie. 'I don't know if you can hear me. I don't know if you're listening at all. But we need back up. We need warm blankets. We need hot chocolate, goddamn it! And we need a team down the river. A body is moving down the river. Correction, two   bodies are moving down the river. I don't know if you can hear me, but we need help-'

The walkie-talkie beeped.

'Loud and clear, Inspector. Two cars are almost there. Just hang on. Over.'

Frigg was crying. She'd once said that she didn't feel anything at all. Now she seemed to be feeling everything. All of the pent-up emotions. Everything that had bothered her, for years and years. All of the anger and hatred and humiliation and pain and fear.

But, for all that, the one great emotion she felt was relief.

She felt forgiven. She felt relief. Her great burdens had, just for a moment, been lifted.

The Inspector moved closer to her, concerned. She hugged him. The two embraced, like father and daughter, and waited for the police to arrive.

Epilogue

Inspector Todor

They pulled Tasha's body out just before the falls. Luckily, she was still in one piece. It was different for Todd Morrow. A frozen body going over a waterfall was liable to fracture, no matter how small and picturesque the waterfall. A team would be required to find all the parts of him.

But Tasha was in one piece. Her body remained miraculously preserved. The undertaker was called upon to perform the autopsy. After washing his hands and saying the prayers he always said prior to such an undertaking, he set to work.

The process took two hours. Inspector Todor sat in Drag's living room, writing up a report of the incidents as he saw them. A little judicious rewriting would, he hoped, cover his most grievous mistakes. Frigg, after all, had been saved. Todd Morrow was dead, which was no victory, but then from another perspective, he was no longer a threat. Overall, Todor felt he'd done well.

Frigg, or Frigite McBride as the report named her, had been inconsolable. He'd taken her back to her mother's house. A female officer sat with them, drinking hot chocolate. She attempted to console her, but Frigg was too broken up. A specialist was required, really. Inspector Todor requested one in his report.

He hoped that by the time the report was read, the snow would have finally stopped falling. The roads into town might've cleared again. Until that happened, nobody was getting in or out of Avon Murray, no matter the emergency.

Frigg would have to find some way to cope. The way they'd all have to.

After a couple of hours, the undertaker stepped out of his mortuary, snapping the gloves from his hands and stared down at Inspector Todor with world weary eyes.

Todor looked up.

'What is it?'

The mortician rubbed his hands together and sighed.

'Your initial theorem, about the murder,' he said. 'It was not accurate.'

'Not accurate?'

'Before I offer my humble opinion, I remind you that I am only an undertaker. I am not trained in criminal post-mortem, only the regular kind. Nevertheless, I believe that this unfortunate event was nothing but a simple accident.'

Todor stared at the undertaker, his mouth agape.

'But... everyone confessed? Everyone!'

'That is most peculiar, yes.'

Drag nodded and walked to the window.

'But the body, Inspector, it shows no signs of struggle. In

fact, the death it describes is a blissful one. Unfortunate in one so young, yes, but of all the ways to go, surely one to be envied.'

Todor leaned against a counter.

'What do you mean? How could it be?'

'A simple fall,' Drąg said. 'That's what I believe anyway. The only damage to the girl's body occurs at the back of the skull. It is a severe and deep trauma, consistent with falling backwards. There was no other mark on her.

'From what I can see, she was walking home, perhaps from a meeting with the Farringdon boy – they live around there, yes? – and as she went up over that humpbacked bridge, she slipped. Her skull was cracked before she even knew what was happening. The look on her face is one of total calm. A blissful state. Perhaps she was still dreaming of him, or having any number of young and hopeful dreams, when it all ended. It happened too fast for her to even tell what was happening.'

Inspector Todor scratched his chin. What did that mean? His every move, every decision; it'd all been in order to find a killer who never existed.

'But, what about the confessions? There were so many! And then, at the end, the boy who lived in the woods had that girl. I saw it myself, there was murder in his eyes!'

'Perhaps you saved her,' Drąg nodded, his voice old and heavy. 'Perhaps it is good that the boy is dead. God can take the sinner sometimes prior to the sin. All I'm telling you, is that Todd Morrow did not kill that girl beneath the ice. Nobody did.'

'I don't understand,' Todor said, collapsing back into the chair.

'It's too much. All of this running around. Too much for it just to end this way. All the lying, heating, and backstabbing that went on. The whole village in uproar…'

'It is always the way,' Drąg shrugged. 'And a sad thing too. Human beings are not rational creatures, Inspector. Surely your years have taught you that? Surely every crime is based on such feelings? Guilt. Sin. The intolerable burdens of our living on this Earth.'

'So, the Barcrofts and the Farringdons?' Todor asked.

'Two families who have long despised each other, from what I hear. Each one seeing their own flaws in the other. And there is nothing that makes people sicker, spiritually ill, like seeing their own flaws.'

'How do you know that?'

Drąg looked at Todor. The ancient, pessimistic mask hinted at pity.

'The town talks, Inspector. You should listen to it sometimes. The townspeople are filled with pettiness, yes… but then so is our existence.'

The Inspector nodded, lying back in Drąg's old couch and feeling the cushions swallow him up. He wished they would swallow him whole. Let him disappear, away from this life into some quiet zone of comfort.

'The decomposition, for example,' Drąg said. 'I was wrong about its mystery. I am an old man and I get carried away sometimes, God forgive me. If she went into the water dead then the freeze would be near instant. She would be like a blackberry in liquid nitrogen. Perfectly preserved.'

Drąg sighed, mournfully.

'I place too much trust in the supernatural, it seems.'

Todor thought of the Farringdons. William, the patriarch. Would he stick it out in his house on the hill? He'd care for his wife in the only way he knew how, which was to put up with her when he could, and to avoid her for the rest. Farringdon's wife, Helen, would no doubt die soon. Such was the intention of all alcoholics; to manage a slow disappearing. An exit from the world so gradual that the soul leaves long before the body finally perishes.

The son, Lucas, would leave. As soon as possible, Todor knew, the boy would go to the city. The daughter had done the same. The insular nature of a small town was bitter when one was under its suspicion, and even after the police pronounced the death an accident, the townspeople would still, no doubt, keep blaming Lucas for the death.

Mrs Barcroft's daughter, Jen, would leave as well. Returning to her life in the city. Not a wholesome existence, certainly, but a life which fit her in a way that Avon Murray never could.

That would leave Mrs Barcroft. Still in charge of the school and living alone. She and William. Two big figures in the old mold. Physically and emotionally barricaded against the changing world. She, up in her headteacher's tower. He, in his house high in the valley. Like eagles, proud and hungry.

'And you, Inspector?' Drąg asked. 'What do you think

will happen to you?'

'I don't know,' Todor shrugged. 'I honestly don't. Part of me thinks I should've never started this policing business. I've been a sham, a two-bit actor, my entire life. But here I am. I can do no other.'

Drąg walked over to the slumped Inspector. He sat next to him, placing a hand on his shoulder.

'We have all sinned,' Drąg said, his voice still tired, as if by the ages. 'But where there is life, there is hope. You might be a terrible police officer, Inspector, but you are a good man. Let the one be the making of the other.'

He stood up and paced slowly back towards his mortuary.

'And stop feeling so bloody sorry for yourself. It's pathetic.'

'Maybe I'll get a dog,' Todor said. 'At least he won't judge me.'

'Do!'

Inspector Todor sniffed, picking up his report and tapping his finger against it. He folded the papers under his arm, walked to the door, saw the snow was still falling, and left.

Thanks for reading The Girl Beneath the Ice, if you enjoyed the book please consider leaving a review.

Visit www.Northodox.co.uk for more northern crime fiction.

Acknowledgements

Thank you to the good people at Northodox Press for taking on the book, and for James' keen editorial eye in particular. There is a huge amount of work that goes on behind the scenes, and this book is really a team effort.

Thanks to the Nexus Writers' Group - especially Karen and Hannah - for your great feedback and for keeping me going. It's a shame they closed down our venue.

A special thanks is owed to Morag Rose, whose lecture at the Manchester Gothic Conference introduced me to the "Manchester Ice Maiden" story, from which this novel took its inspiration. The Loiterer's Resistance Movement does great work in keeping the old stories alive, and discovering new ones.

Thanks to Steve Hanson, my co-editor at the Manchester Review of Books, whose own prolific output I often use to excuse my own. If Steve can write that many good books back-to-back, surely I can too.

Finally, thank you to my friends and family, who were always supportive - even during my experimental phase - and continue to say nice things about my work. And to Kinga, to whom this book, like my life, is dedicated.

NORTHODOX PRESS

HOME OF NORTHERN VOICES

 FACEBOOK.COM/NORTHODOXPRESS

 TWITER.COM/NORTHODOXPRESS

 INSTAGRAM.COM/NORTHODOXPRESS

 NORTHODOX.CO.UK

SUBMISSIONS ARE OPEN!

WRITER &
DEBUT AUTHOR [ ]

NOVELS &
SHORT FICTION [ ]

FROM OR LIVING
IN THE NORTH [ ]